DISRUPTED GEARS

DISRUPTED GEARS

NELSON MCKEEBY

4 Horsemen
Publications, Inc.

4 Horsemen
Publications, Inc.

4 Horsemen Publications, Inc.
1497 Main St. Suite 169
Dunedin, FL 34698
4horsemenpublications.com
info@4horsemenpublications.com

Cover & Typesetting by Autumn Skye
Edited by Laura Mita

Library of Congress Control Number: 2023940015

Paperback ISBN-13: 979-8-8232-0238-1
Hardcover ISBN-13: 979-8-8232-0240-4
Audiobook ISBN-13: 979-8-8232-0237-4
Ebook ISBN-13: 979-8-8232-0239-8

Dedicated to Sir Galahad, Isabeau, and Philipe, cats, and friends.

TABLE OF CONTENTS

RAINS-A-LOT AND IVY

DATE: JULY 22, 1960
LOCATION: CLEVELAND, GEORGIA

Ivy looked out of the front windows into the green Georgian miasma of fetid summer. The house he was in was a southern colonial with a wraparound front porch, one floor and proper, with a yellow picket fence, exuberant pansy-flowers planted in ranks by a cement walkway all the more absurd because the main road had no pavement, and the house lacked indoor facilities. His eyes darted around taking in data that he had missed, coming in from the back entrance, Browning drawn, his partner at his back like a guardian spirit.

The window was meticulously clean. The porch was neat with wooden furniture and a green pie cooling rack. A small fragment of carpet on the ground before the door said, "Welcome!" in Spencerian script. The yard was trimmed closely, and a manual mower was sitting under a pecan tree where it had been left in mid-chore, a testament to unfinished work.

Ivy stepped out onto the porch of the double-wide trailer and saw what he had come out for. A plate of pie had been left to cool on a pie rack made of green enameled metal and small, round, porcelain trays which were fitted with elaborate hinges, allowing them to be lifted up and folded flat against the pie rack's vertical rear scaffold. The reason the trays should be designed to collapse was not evident as the pie cooler essentially took the same amount of space with them raised or lowered. It was just an illogical variance of mundane existence that presented itself to a person used to looking at the world through the panopticon of a mental Fresnel lens. The fact was observed and noted as sinister, outrageous, or indicative, depending on how much scotch one had consumed during the day. You could question the motives of the pie rack maker in putting the effort into hinging the problematic pie plate holders, or question the motives of the universe for being a place where pie rack hinges could take on looming portents of existential dread. Or he could take things through the side entrance and see that the green enamel of the pie cooling rack was the real issue, its deep forest shade reminiscent of the uniform of a German sniper that bedeviled him years and thousands of kilometers away in space/time, whose dead eyes were shot out by an African sergeant in United States twill, the bravest man he had ever met, his name forgotten in the slide of time.

And then there was the plate of pie covered daintily with a silky gauze of muslin to allow it to cool without flies or excess condensation. The presence of the white cloth sitting on what was probably an acceptable homemade pie was like a comb brushed on a chalkboard of the imagination. So mundane but so rapacious in its meaning, it made Ivy want to fall on his knees and scream a rage-filled rant, loud and caustic and made from mostly unfolded consonants barked in staccato dissonance at the sky. Outwardly, he nodded at the pie and listened to the humming of the power line that led into the house above the porch and to the flitting dance of bottle flies above the screened door, bloated and horrible in their digestive process. The mendacity and the horror curled together into a symphony around his being.

The pie in question turned out to be pecan.

Lifting the cloth and placing it on the tray above was a second of trivial action that expressed itself in the ether like a puff of white clouds. The cloth was a complex math problem, each second being tossed by wind, his hands, angry blowflies feeding on gore, or a million other variables that tugged potential in every direction. A true European would not have made the identification of the pie beneath the cloth on top of the doily that rested on the porcelain disk that was attached to the metal frame, which the creator of the rack had designed to be hinged and maddening in its mobility. Ivy was no longer truly European and had slowly allowed American culture into his spirit, and despite his partner's rejection of the American trope, it was inevitable that living and working among the people of the United States would affect him, like smoke affected a ham in a smokehouse.

The owner of the house who sat inside the living room on a brocade loveseat next to her husband, just a few meters away from the pie cooling outside, had made the sweet in question that morning with an idea that it should be consumed at the most opportune time: right when it had shed the oven heat but before it had spent a night withering in the humid southern heat. In other words, it was ready now, just waiting for a human or some other animal with a sweet tooth to come by and appreciate it.

Ivy rubbed his neck. The heat caused the leather straps that ran behind his back under his charcoal-gray Madison and Rigby suit, with its absurd built-up shoulder pieces that made him look like a triangle, to ride against his skin and shirt, creating a place that collected sweat and making it uncomfortably clammy. Then he reached for a fancy pie fork that was laid out on a side table for company, and he carefully maneuvered a piece from its pie tin and placed it on a blue and white porcelain plate. Ivy had spoken to the woman just an hour before, telling her to prepare for his arrival. Most people Ivy warned about his arrival would be endeavoring to leave by the rear exit, but not the woman on the phone. She thanked Ivy with a tinkle of Bible verses and said he was welcome to the wonderful ice tea, wonderful because her husband knew just what amount of love was appropriate to place in each liter of pungent liquid. In her rapid talk, she mentioned lunch and a pie. Evidently, the pie she mentioned was one from the preternatural pie rack whose enameled shade was that of a dead sniper's tunic. He remembered the man, long forgotten by Ivy, he was a German killed by a Black tanker when Ivy was just 15. He shook off the horrors of his youth and turned his attention back to the pie. Carefully, Ivy pulled his jackknife from his pocket, opened its largest blade, and incised a cut into the confection from its geographic center to its rim. A second cut produced what Americans called a slice. In this case, a slice meant a triangle about 300 grams in mass representing 16% of the pie's mass. He selected a fork from a small pile and proceeded inside.

With his pie secured, Ivy entered the house and immediately found his partner Rains-a-Lot standing flat-footed, a long telescoping metal radio antenna in his hands. The Indian was looking closely at a large mezuzah hanging from the door jamb. The enameled wooden icon was open, and Rains-a-Lot had removed a piece of parchment from it. The parchment did not seem to disturb him though. It was that the icon had been hung crooked on the door jam. He stared at the object, concentration radiating from his black hair and his handsome wind-burned face, asking himself why was this not straight.

Ivy let Rains-a-Lot contemplate the mezuzah. The pie was tugging at him, so he cradled the plate in one hand and took a bite with the other using the fancy service fork made from real silver. The modish silver fork was a contemporary piece by Adda Husted-Andersen with her crossed stick-like engraving on the handle. It functioned properly, and the pie filled his mouth with a sweet, savory flavor, the crunch of nuts and the shortening of the crust setting each other off.

Rains-a-Lot brought his car antenna up, closed his eyes, and scanned the religious icon. He then looked again at the paper. *"Barukh atah Adonai Eloheinu melekh ha'olam, asher qideshanu bemitzvotav vetzivanu liqboa,"* Ivy said to him, "It protects the door from evil."

Ivy watched as the Indian left the icon behind, folded the wrap of paper up like it was a magical relic, and placed it in his leather jacket. Rains-a-Lot was oddly spiritual and attuned to the mystical world, as if his story was told in not one but two worlds, and this one was the least important. They both worked for Dustin-Rhodes Corporation, but Rains-a-Lot was an old-timer with a past and a legend. His largest personality trait was his taciturn nature. Of all the Troubleshooters in the Operations division, Rains-a-Lot was the best, but few agents could handle his constant assessing way and his lack of verbosity. Ivy though not only accepted it but also embraced it. His own ghosts could drive him to speech or shut him up, and Rains-a-Lot did not care. Rains-a-Lot cared only if someone was competent. He did not understand cowardice because he had none himself. Unlike most agents, Rains-a-Lot ate frugal meals, drank no alcohol, and did not gamble, and his frustrations were not peevish. Although he was a beautiful man, looking like Jay Silverheels with a strong, kind face, glittering eyes alive with charisma, and a spare frame of rippling muscles that allowed him to move gracefully and naturally in a mesmeric way, he never chased women. Except for an odd taste in hats and a love of movies, he rejected Western culture to the point that he did not drive automobiles. Ivy was not sure he could.

Ivy ate another bite of pie and watched as Rains-a-Lot slowly walked around the living room of the house with a car's radio antenna in his hand prosecuting his investigation. It was too early in the day to start down one of those esoteric paths, which only made sense once serious drinking could start after five o'clock, but the Indian seemed to sense something, and if his radio antenna was a bit of vaudeville being called up as part of his ongoing effort to poke humor at a strictly rational universe, it was serving some practical purpose.

Rains-a-Lot's path crossed Ivy, and he looked into his partner's eyes. Ivy offered Rains-a-Lot the pie softly, and the Indian shook his head. Ivy shrugged and returned his head to the door frame, shaking off the foul odor that was trying to make itself known in the corner of his mind.

Rains-a-Lot stopped walking and stared at Ivy, radiating an unusual distress, and looked at the pie. Ivy replied to his partner by saying, "Seems the guest said no to a slice of pie."

Rains-a-Lot nodded grimly. "How many symptoms do you need to declare the rain is made of water?" his face asked silently. If the Indian was, in Ivy's experience, guarded even on the best of days, he was downright taciturn now. Unlike Ivy, Rains-a-Lot wore a bomber jacket of leather, pleated cloth pants, a cotton shirt, and a strange-looking straw boater cap, so at least he was comfortable... and to hell with corporate regulations.

Ivy placed the pie plate, encumbered with the Adda Husted-Andersen silver fork and the remains of his slice of pie, onto a Montgomery Wards television tray sitting at the back of the room. There were four trays. Two were in front of the owners of the house. One was placed in front of a smaller but very comfortable lounge chair. The last had been taken out and left unused. He turned then and looked at the owners of the house. They shared a beautiful loveseat, clutching each other tightly, eyes wide open, but did not look directly at Ivy or Rains-a-Lot at any point. They were frozen in fear, caught in the second. Ivy noticed a fresh glass of tea sitting in front of the woman, sweating moisture in the heat. He walked over to her and stared into her eyes for a second, then took the glass. It contained a light tea and was filled to the brim, which included a few centimeters of eroded ice. Ivy looked deeply in the glass and saw no discoloration, so he sipped deeply of the drink. He almost spit it out, but powered through the taste and set the glass down. Rains-a-Lot was staring at Ivy in thought just as Ivy had stared at him.

"Sugar tea," Ivy said. Rains-a-Lot allowed his gaze to fall on the couple in the loveseat before returning it back to Ivy. He then walked over to where two other glasses sat on the ground. He picked one up, ran his finger inside, and tasted the remaining liquid. Ivy said, "Water?" Rains-a-Lot nodded.

Ivy contemplated the second glass, empty, which had rolled beneath the lamp stand. "My bet is the third glass had water as well." Now Rains-a-Lot nodded.

Ivy turned to the couple and said, a polite smile sketching his face, "You probably do not drink alcohol, but you like sweet things." He turned and slowly walked to the kitchen, measuring each step like it was a loan from Mother Earth that would need to be paid back. The room was spotless except for a puddle of water on the floor. Ivy knelt and felt the water. It was cool and clean, like you'd feel on a glacier. He stood up and rubbed his finger on a counter. No grease came up with his finger. Someone scrubbed this place clean often enough that they did not use heavy chemicals. He noted a bottle of Simple Green on the counter.

The stove was a gas retrofit with four burners. Three burners were empty, but a fourth had a copper pot with liquid in it. The pot was warm, the savory liquid was deep red in color and looked fresh. Ivy wondered for a second. The pot held about six liters, a tidy sum, but it was one-twelfth full, and about a half of a liter remained.

Ivy turned and noted an icebox. It was old-fashioned, with a small compressor that kept the whole contraption at five or six degrees, not enough to make ice but enough to keep three or four blocks solid for a week. He opened the larger, lower compartment, and he noted it was cool. He opened the upper compartment. There was no ice. As he turned, he noted four labels from Campbell's condensed tomato soup had been placed into a small hamper attached to the refrigerator by a magnet. He plucked a label from the hamper. Each can was about 250 milliliters in volume, whatever absurd measurement they used in these kitchens here. The instructions in crisp, bitter English called for a can of soup and a can of water, making a hearty meal of savory soup. One-half of a liter of soup each times four cans equals two liters.

He opened the small silver drawer and noted they owned more Adda Husted-Andersen spoons. He had seen their mates in the living room. Ivy closed his eyes and imagined ghosts. He pulled a small silver knife from the drawer. "How much do you imagine custom silver is worth?" he asked loudly. There was a grunt from Rains-a-Lot in the other room.

He rubbed the silver and imagined its maker, an artisan in New York, not so long ago, pouring the silver form, cooling it, checking it for voids, then punching and polishing the implement, at once valuable for metal as it was useful for separating butter from a stick and spreading it on cornbread. The butter cool from the icebox, the cornbread hot from the oven and begging for consumption like a suicidal fish that jumps in your boat. It was a compelling image that haunted Ivy.

Silver was 25 cents a gram. So this beautiful knife, melted cruelly down, was worth two dollars to an opium fiend in some Atlanta shooting den, a full hit of his beloved black tar shot into his veins by Vinny Psycho on Peach Street. The set of treasured silver had 80 pieces in it and massed 2 kilograms. Drug-using criminals were known for their respect for family heirlooms. They always left the silver.

He looked deeper into the drawer. There was a paper inside that said, “Kelle will need to know this.” The writing was Spencerian script, and the paper was card stock. Ivy placed the card in his pocket, not knowing it would change his life.

He closed his eyes. Thoughts were things you fish from the lake made rough by the weather of emotions and sentiment. He saw the woman’s beloved silver, not old but purchased from hoarded money before even a water closet. That made sense. The couple and their house were a neat logical package, floating in the waters of time. The doting husband had no need for a bathroom when he had water in the kitchen, a well-built privy, and the shining light of his wife’s eyes as she laid out her silver to break their fast Saturday evening.

Ivy opened his eyes again and saw the vision had been an overlooked detail. The man had a picture on the wall of him with a huge fish, a Kodachrome moment of victory. Ivy turned suddenly, but his danger-sense turned out to be Rains-a-Lot, who had come into the kitchen as well. His metal rod pointed at the picture of the fish as well.

Ivy asked, "Would you have taken soup?" The Indian looked again at the picture then nodded and turned back for the family room. He would have indeed had soup. They both would.

Alone again, Ivy continued his spiritual journey through the kitchen. There was a cupboard by the stove. The cupboard was perfect with sturdy handles and well-made wood finished in green, and it was smartly carved. It was an old piece cared for and maintained despite being worked hard each day. He opened it. Inside were six dinner plates, six bread plates, and two large soup bowls. They were a set made by Montgomery Ward and ordered as a fixed unit. Ivy took one of the large bowls and placed it on his head. It fit quite well. His foot then kicked something beneath the cupboard.

Ivy went down to his knees, one hand holding the soup bowl on his head. Beneath the cupboard were several boxes of groceries, neatly stored items that the kitchen owner did not often use. There were a box of empty Atlas Jars on a small wooden stick, a second container of jars filled with produce, being protected from light damage in this dark nook, and a 24-bottle, wooden delivery tray of Red Budwine, a soda pop common in the area. One bottle was not quite lined up correctly. Ivy nudged it with his finger, and it dropped into place. He looked at the bottle, then grabbed it up and stood.

He imagined the couple. They liked pie and made it for themselves, and they shared it with people who came to see them. They did not like soda themselves, but their grandkids did. So when they visited, did you feed them RC Cola from the store, sugar and caffeine to send them crazy into orbit, or did you give them Budwine, bought in the drugstore and reputed to have health benefits? The Budwine was kept for the grandkids and offered to any guests who might seem as though they would like that sort of drink.

Ivy had a vision. It was too hard to turn into a phrase, being just a wisp that could fade away if saddled with leather words and whipped into a frenzy of sentences and paragraphs. Three portions of soup. Pie untouched. Soda offered but refused. Water! Oh, you were thirsty. Of course, you needed to drink it all. Greedy for water. Ivy turned back to rejoin Rains-a-Lot.

As he walked back into the living room, a Ford Model A with a wind-blown man driving it roared to a stop in front of the house. Rains-a-Lot looked up from his busy work, folded up his little car antenna, and drew his Smith and Wesson Model 3 from under his jacket. Ivy waved him back down and said, "It's only Charlie." Time seemed to unroll a little faster now that the courier had arrived.

Charlie. Almost two meters and under 50 kilos, he looked like a flamingo had swallowed a dolphin head first. He was a study of almost. His almost bald head appeared almost completely covered in sweat, while his huge glasses almost allowed him to see well enough to make out of almost anyone's face before they could almost touch him. He was wearing a Charcoal suit just like Ivy, but his body was not designed for even well-tailored clothing. The suit almost fit him as well as it would have fit a brown bear. Charlie carried a big magnum revolver on his belt that had somehow dropped down onto the back of his pants, which were being pulled to half-mast by the weapon's weight, almost low enough that the canyon was occasionally reaching the sinkhole of his personal geography. He was almost a character from some French comedy movie. If there had been any stealth to him, he could have been a mime.

And of course, like most agents of Dustin-Rhodes Corporation, he was a conundrum of "How did recruiting ever find someone like that?" Charlie was almost as fearless as Ivy, shot almost as well as Rains-a-Lot, and was preternaturally attractive to women. The reason for the last supposedly existed on page 13 of his personal file, but as this page was almost entirely covered in black redaction ink, covering no doubt what was an interesting chapter in human evolution and existence. *Perhaps,* Ivy thought, *women are smarter than men.* He sadly reflected on the women in his life. The women in Steno called him a catch, but he knew that his Gallic looks and saturnine cast were just water that covered a dark mirror. He was not intentionally cruel, but life threw him around and did not protect the people he loved. He could imagine Charlie being a fierce defender of his mate, like the hairless bear he resembled.

Charlie tripped as he came out of the Model A, recovered, and then dragged from the back seat two large buckets filled with something cold. He turned to the house, almost tripped on his face when was negotiating the stairs, ran into the door jamb as he tried to open it without putting down the buckets first, and finally, succeeded in entering. He came to a halt in the room, staring at the household owner and his wife.

"Jesus Christ," he said.

Ivy shook his head. "Not sure that name applies." He glanced at the mezuzah and back at Charlie.

"Their heads have been sawn off," Charlie exclaimed.

Ivy replied, "Technically their skullcaps have been removed from the top of their skulls."

"Did you put their skullcaps on the dinner trays?" he asked.

"No, that was someone else," Ivy said.

"Wendigo," Rains-a-Lot opined, watching Charlie closely. One theory around the office was that Charlie was going to go berserk one day and start shooting when someone had filled him with too much crazy. The idea was that the 20 questions you always played with Charlie around strange investigations were like a sputtering wick, and every wick has to end sometime. Rains-a-Lot, Ivy knew, had money bet on the exact outcome. Ivy knew the Indian did not consider it gambling.

Ivy shrugged. A Wendigo was a myth. Superstition. This was science: a fact.

Charlie put down his buckets. "The blood in the skull caps?"

"Tomato soup by Campbells," Ivy replied. "One can is missing by-the-by. One can went into each skull, and another is on the stove."

Rains-a-Lot stopped his pacing and narrowed his eyes. Ivy nodded at him, as if to say, "You do the math." Rains-a-Lot rubbed his hand on his forehead. It was not like he would miss Ivy wearing a soup bowl in place of his pork pie hat. Ivy puffed up his cheeks and looked up, saying to Rains-a-Lot, "Just what you think."

Charlie was sputtering like a tea kettle, drawing their attention from their private conversation to him. "And the brains?" he finally croaked.

Ivy stepped closer. "That is the interesting point." He pulled out a pen light and flashed it on the woman's still nose. "They were breathing when someone..."

"Wendigos," Rains-a-Lot added.

Ivy shot back, "Someone ... snaked a sharp object that could make 40- to 60-degree angle changes into the brain cavity, and another similar object that could cauterize blood vessels and slurp out blood. The skull cap was removed, then the cerebellum was cut out in a series of 29 cuts for each person. Then someone put a serving of tomato soup in the skulls. Afterward, they left, and we arrived 19 minutes later." Ivy waited for Charles to notice the only bowl in the room was sitting on his head. He did not notice.

Charlie said, "They are still close?"

Ivy nodded. "Very close."

"And the buckets?" Charlie asked. "You asked for them yesterday?"

Rains-a-Lot pulled a pair of thick thermal gloves from under his jacket and held them up for Ivy, who grabbed them and slipped them on. From the steaming buckets, he moved around what sounded like rocks, then pulled out one human brain, then a second. Each brain he placed into an empty skull cavity. He then dumped the soup from the skull caps. Rains-a-Lot threw him a tube of epoxy, which he used to fix each of the skull caps to their respective heads. Ivy stepped back and said, "Natural causes."

Charlie threw up a meal of meatloaf, mashed potatoes, and collards.

After cleaning up Charlie's vomit and seeing him back to his car, Ivy and Rains-a-Lot took off in their Chevy. Rains-a-Lot was looking out the window as they drove down the red-brown clay drive. Ivy reached out and patted his shoulder. The Indian was angry; Ivy could tell by the set of his shoulders, the way he looked about, the creases in his forehead, and the way he set his jaw. He was angry at losing the bet with Ivy on what they would find in the house, angry at having arrived only a few minutes too late to prevent the murder, and angrier still that the deaths had been an old retired couple who made pie and soup for guests.

Ivy watched as the hills went by, the motorway turning from red clay path to brown dirt road to gray byway, the sleepy spell of summer blowing past, and the sounds of the south playing. Rains-a-Lot started to take out a map, but Ivy waved it away. He could do the math and had seen the maps before they started out. And now, with the mystery solved, it was just a case of talking to locals and finding a scent to lead them to their target.

Ivy saw the road he was looking for, Lake Street. The lake in question was a largish, snaking body of water built by the TVA for power and recreation in this region 20 years ago. Now that the trees had returned and the government-bought land had gone wild, Northern Georgia was actually quite pretty. He drove down the winding road and thought this would be a pretty place to live, here on the edge of the mountains, a million miles from Atlanta. You could hide here, buy a home, find work in a forge or conservation lot, grow scraggly vegetables, and drink your memories away. If it got too boring, you could grab the scattergun from above the door and pull off your work boots and your darned socks and use your toes to fire little lead satellites into space.

Rains-a-Lot whistled and sat up. Ivy slowed down and asked, "You have something?"

The Indian nodded and put his fist in a ball to his lips. After a second, he blew on his fist, and his finger came out pointing to a twist in the road ahead. A young teen was pulling a red garden cart along. In the cart were fishing supplies, camping gear, and some wooden boxes. Ivy commented, "All too easy, no?"

Rains-a-Lot nodded.

They pulled over by the side of the road after passing the teenager. A cloud of dust that had been following them for five minutes caught up all at once and formed little cyclones of brack around them, eddies of gray- and red-colored micro-particles that were the primary export of the region, after corn liquor and stick-built furniture.

The boy was a lanky teen, lacking shoes, wearing blue coveralls, a red shirt, a straw hat, and a parti-color scarf. His skin was red from the sun, freckled, and fiery. He had blond hair that had been poorly cut by blunt scissors, the type that would tear at a scalp rather than truly saw through hair and left one numb from the tonsorial chores. Ivy had always thought such scissors and their carnage were a French invention of the Oblates or perhaps the Carthusian, but perhaps they had been adopted by the Baptists in this strange land as well. The boy turned his head ponderously to glare at Ivy and said, "Won't talk to no cruddy injun."

Ivy got out of the car. "You do not have to, master?"

"Naah. None of that. You carbet-bags can haul up out. If you thinking I will be just giving you my true name, you can sit on a stick," the boy drawled.

Rains-a-Lot got out of the car with a great deal of care-worn menace. Ivy glanced at him as he came around the purple Chevy, tapping its metal top with his fingers. The Chevy was a great vehicle, but it needed to feel in the loop otherwise it would not run its best. It liked human touch in a friendly way. Rains-a-Lot stopped and leaned on the car, staring at the kid.

"You do not scare me, rooster," the kid said.

"I have no intention of scaring you. How about I call you Jim?" Ivy reached into his back pocket and pulled out the bottle of Budwine secreted there. He prized the cap off with his thumb and finger and offered it. "Care for a soda?"

"Doan go in for sweets kicker," the kid angrily replied.

Ivy smirked. He allowed his eyes to look at each detail of the kid's skin and clothes, then said, *"An íocann an t-iascach do pháiste pá an loch?"*

"Cad a fhios agat faoi rígh an iascaigh?" The teen replied in a clean guttural growl. Then there was a second of realization. "The Wizard will gut you!" The child then said.

Ivy found himself standing by a small woman with dark hair in a princess or queen's gown. The dress was brocaded and luxurious with small star sapphires and mountain pearls worked into the green and blue fabric. They were looking at a young city, a place being built clinker style with pegs and boards, on foundations of quarry stone. She places his hand in hers and says, "You look lost."

"I was once attacked by a Child-of-the-Lake, and before they kill you and feast on your blood, they give you a view of the future that they are stealing from you," Ivy said to her. His heart felt large in his chest as he felt her touch his hand.

"In the magical lands?" she asked. "Is this where the beast attacked you?

He shook his head. "Earth."

The woman held him a little closer, a command for him to embrace her back. He did so with pleasure. She looked up into his face and said, "And if they only bestow this gift before they devour you, what is the secret to you being here now?"

A laugh came from behind him. He turned, and it was a woman with dark skin in a purple dress, her eyes glowing in the darkness. "The answer to your riddle, my Queen, is that you do not agree to die!"

A loud explosion shattered his skull, or that is what it felt like. Ivy collapsed to his knees with weakness, but he was able to draw his Browning from the leather holster under his jacket. It was not needed. Before him, the teen stood, eyes staring dumbly at a metal bowl that he had removed from Ivy's head. His fingers turned long with sharp ends steaming with acid. His jaw was outthrust, and his shoulders spread out a little. His freckles and red face were now a solid dull pink color, and slits formed in his neck.

A third eye had opened in the teen's head where Rains-a-Lot had sent a 10-gram bolus of lead propelled by black powder into the creature's brain. The Child-of-the-Lake slowly collapsed in on himself and vibrated in death, its skin bubbling a little from some inner heat. Rains-a-Lot sat Ivy down in the driver's seat of the purple Chevy, which wrapped her emotional arms around him, so all he had to do was watch the Indian work and take calm sips from the bottle of blood-red soda. First, the body of the Child-of-the-Lake went into a lined stainless steel trunk. Then Rains-a-Lot retrieved two human brains from paired Montgomery Ward soup bowls that were hidden in wooden boxes in the cart and carefully put them into cooling canisters. To catch a Fisher King, one must have brains harvested by a Child-of-the-Lake, and now they had bait for a fishing trip.

DELBERT'S DILEMMA

DATE: AUGUST 13, 1960
LOCATION: 41.4083, −122.1972, (CALIFORNIA)

Delbert watched as Richard Todd Hamblin and Benjamin Day huddled around an oil heater at the edge of Shasta Base Camp. He was officially the Senior Troubleshooter, Executive Division. If Dustin-Rhodes was a corporation that accomplished things at a price, then the Troubleshooters were the point of the sharpest knife in the drawer. Failure was never an option, and the men and women he employed were known for two things, competence and the willingness to do what was needed to complete a task.

And now he was called to put out a five-alarm fire. In the executive contract files, one of the oddest standing orders the company had was 11060. Delbert held the mimeograph of that very contract in his hand.

> Upon location of K-sub BRAINERD, KELLE (file 11060-A70) return individual via office stop 70 to client designated BRAINTRUST (file 11060-A1). Payment Class Z.

The contract on its face seemed simple. If a young woman shows up in your neck of the woods, grab her without violence, protect her person beyond all costs, and deliver her to their lab in Wyoming run by Dr. Preston Arneveldt.

Not so simple it turns out. All evidence showed his two best Troubleshooters had driven the subject of the contract into the maw of a tornado. Not only had they disappeared, but also an entire town had been leveled by the tornado they had driven into.

It was pretty easy to cover up some things. Take this spot right here. There were always strange things going on around these mountains. People would disappear and reappear. Tall alien-like creatures would show up and have dinner at a local restaurant. Short, heavily bearded men would be seen stealing a backhoe from a local construction sight. It was like the universe channeled its crazy through this single mountain, and over the years, Dustin-Rhodes had received dozens of contracts to explore, exploit, or cover up some aspects of the mountain's odd existence.

Dustin-Rhodes Corporation was, at the end of the day, a company that did things for people. That was it. Someone came to Dustin Rhodes and defined a problem. Dustin Rhodes then took a hand in finding a solution, if one could be found.

Every contract Dustin Rhodes took on was guaranteed as much as success as was possible to guarantee. If you had come to the company and asked for one million apple pies, then the company had someone in its ranks who would do the math and figure out how long it would take to plant apple trees, collect supplies, rent bakeries, develop and test formulas, and then actually make the pies, and at what cost per kilogram. If that same person wanted the company to solve for pi (π), then the company would quote a cost per hour of labor, set up a division, and start working on the final answer. The client would pay the freight and be given a properly written contract; the client was always right.

The Troubleshooters were the ultimate expression of this. Occasionally, the universe created—through breeding, training, and experience—an extraordinary person. Olympic teams were made up of physical examples of this. Nobel laureates were often intellectual examples of this concept. With Troubleshooters, they were people who solved problems, no matter what those problems were. Currently, after looking through the entire world, only 39 people qualified as Troubleshooters.

Delbert tested millions of people to find one that could handle the work. They did not fail often, and when it seemed they had failed, it was either because the universe had conspired against them and they had been asked to handle an impossible task or because failure to carry out their assigned mission was actually success at carrying out what should have been their assigned mission.

He was surrounded by a vastness of white snow and blue sky with the occasional gray rock sticking through. Standing on the top of Mount Shasta, freezing his nuts off, Delbert kept telling himself that whatever Rains-a-Lot and Ivy d'Seille had done, it was the best that could be done in the circumstances. The company had a responsibility to communicate to their client that the contract had hit a snag and ask for instructions on how to proceed, which opened up this frozen can of worms. Finding out the client was in Madagascar and would require a service team of 6,000 pilots, sailors, ground supply people, and radio-telephone operators to open a channel of communication with was nothing unusual. Finding out the client existed in the temporal year of the Common Era 2020, 60 years in the future, was not the usual scenario, it just added a special twist to the problem.

The normal way of communicating with this client was to select a sequential safe deposit box in a bank in Des Moines, one paid up until the year 2200, well past the date when it would be opened, and insert a note. The note was apparently read somewhere in the future and acted upon. Communication backward was more difficult but worked the same way, somehow the future entity had an agent in the past that they had reliable contact with. He or she used Western Union with prepaid delayed wires.

This was hardly a streamlined way of communicating and had distinct limits. It could also collapse if the safe deposit boxes were tampered with, or something happened to the agent in the past. Long, complicated communications required discussions to happen in person. The only easily accessible place by each side was in another universe, at least according to the big brains in Reality Physics. And "easily accessible" was a matter of opinion.

Delbert turned to the fidgeting man standing behind him. "Dr. Arneveldt, I am about three seconds from throwing you off this mountain and taking the negative feedback session with Human Resources. Hell, maybe I will throw your entire team off and take the 30-day anger management seminar, I hear it is being held in Tahiti this year."

"Mr. Devine, there is no need for that sort of talk." The man was clearly nervous, indicating there was indeed a need for that type of talk. He kept looking at an impressive amount of gear rigged up on the mountain. Gear that looked dangerously like a kite rig, something that just might get the good doctor tossed from the top of the mountain.

Not satisfied with his answer, Delbert pulled his hands from his fleece coat and took two steps toward the scientist. "Are you telling me what there is a need of?"

"Please, Mr. Devine." He tried to step back, but he did not fight the hands on his coat.

Delbert gestured toward a group of men in expensive clothing, smoking cigars and drinking from vacuum flasks, heated by a large metal tin device that melted the snow around it and caused rivulets of water to run away and freeze into snaking ice sculptures. "What do you see over there?"

Arneveldt glanced nervously at the figures trying to keep warm by the oil heater but failed to reply. Delbert had found it was wrong to judge men on their visual appearance, but in Arneveldt's case, it would have worked. His popped fish eyes rolled in their sockets like he was a giant walleye, while he tended to use his hands to defend himself like a surprised girl unsure of her right to defend herself from forceful adults.

"Well, what do you see?" Delbert gave him an almost gentle shake.

The walleyes goggled again and rolled around in their sockets, then fixated on the most important of the men. "Mr. Richard Todd Hamblin, sir."

Delbert nodded and put the doctor down, smoothing his parka like he was a recalcitrant kid. "And who else?"

A few seconds pause. "Mr. Benjamin Day… I see Mr. Day!" His voice rose like he had spelled a tough word correctly in a spelling bee.

"Correct. I am glad you get the yearbook in Wyoming. And you're proposing what, exactly?" Delbert let his voice become calm, almost syrupy.

The doctor relaxed a little. "We do not have a choice, sir, not really."

Delbert smiled and patted the doctor on the shoulder, then moved his mouth by the man's ear. With a preternatural calm he said, "Shut up and answer me Dr. Arneveldt. I am getting into a mood." His voice was silky, like a viper. "I am getting into a mood because you lot never really answer my questions with definitive answers, which makes me want to start demoting people. And you know the type of demotion I am talking about?"

The doctor looked at the endless sky past the edge of the mountain and nodded, his prominent Adam's apple bobbing in his neck like a duck looking for seed.

The doctor spent a second pulling himself together. "There are limits to our ability to send objects or people trans-dimensionally. The projection chamber in Wyoming uses a lot of power. The bus bars can only handle a fling of 50 kilograms, and our recharge time with that much mass is 90 hours. It is as much an issue of mathematics as anything else. With better math, we could fling more."

"And the other problem?"

"Yes, sir, it's copper you see. We can't fling it. No idea why." He looked like he was preparing to fly for a second, closing his eyes and saying some sort of prayer.

Delbert said, "And this matters because?"

"It turns out humans have copper in them, and without it, they die." He still had his eyes shut.

Delbert carefully reached up to the man's face and pried open an eyelid. The eyeball underneath rolled in terror. He dropped his hand and asked, "Why?"

Still, with one eye open, he said, "We are looking into that."

Delbert put his hands on his face. Someday, he would retire. He had no illusions about retirement's quality. The company would reward his hard work with exile to some Pacific Island cleaning some war memorial of sedge grass, but he did not care. Counting coconuts for the rest of his life had appeal. Plus, he had developed an eye for the women of the islands during his war service.

Behind his hands, he heard the scientist say, "Mr. Devine, this will work. It has been done dozens of times before."

Delbert remained staring into his palms, thinking about a tropical paradise instead of the top of this damned mountain. "Lay it out for me," he said.

"You, The Big Man, and Mr. Day are tied onto large kites," the scientist said.

God damned you, Delbert thought.

"We then let out your line until you are at a point we have determined as the main temporal transport point. At that point, we send a burst of electricity down your kite wires, and you make a natural transition into the parallel hyperspatial reality." His voice was actually cheery at the prospect.

"Virdea," Delbert said.

"That is a fanciful name sir. It is a hyperspatial congruency, nothing more. There is some theory that your time there is an illusion, a psychological meta-reality."

"You can get shot there?" Delbert asked.

"Oh yes." Arneveldt stood there blinking his eyes at Delbert, ankle-deep in the snow.

"Then forget that psychological meta-reality shit. Every time I get shot, it's no dream. "

"As you say sir."

Delbert put his hands down. "I do say, now how do we get back?"

"Our retreat in Virdea is concealed in a mountaintop temple. When you are ready to return, we have parachutes prepared to make that happen. You parachute off the plateau the temple is built on. Any side. Wait for a flash of light, then pull your chute."

"And where do we end up?"

"Bricktown, New Jersey."

"For fuck's sake." Delbert looked over at his boss. The Big Man was already being fitted onto his kite by the safety crew. The heaviest person who could be taken by kite was 125 kilograms. Both Day and Hamblin pushed that. Delbert was less than 70 kilograms, but he was carrying his toys.

Under his suit coat on his hip, he had a .357 Magnum revolver loaded hot with armor-piercing rounds. Slung from his front, he also had a French MAT-49 submachine gun with six magazines. Portable, deadly firepower. A pochette on his belt had a full medical kit, handcuffs, and a flashlight. In his jacket pocket was a pack of three projectors for 3-quinuclidinyl benzilate. Around his waist was $20,000 all in hundreds.

He watched as his bosses were tied into their machines, then he took the assembly manual and checklist and made damn sure no one had made a mistake. Then, they strapped him into his own kite. The kites were huge four-winged affairs, kept stable by six lines being fed from six cable drums. They were lifted into frames that caught the wind and were launched by simply letting out slack from the drums and throwing a master hook to detach from the frame.

They reeled him into the air, and it was anything but gentle. Despite wearing headgear and a helmet, it was deafening, and the wind gusts needed all six cables to keep the kite turned properly into the wind. If two cables simultaneously parted, he would be left spinning like a record in the sky until the rest of the cables stressed and failed. Then, he would be propelled into the side of the mountain at 200 mph.

At what he hoped was the proper point, he heard the humming that said electricity was being fed into the rig. His hair stood on end, and then there was a gut-wrenching feeling of the wings releasing him, an unexpected development. He fell about 8 feet onto a marble floor, vowing the whole way down to kill Arteveldt as soon as he could.

The Big Man and the Executive Vice President did not seem fazed. They simply picked themselves off the ground and brushed dirt from their puffy jackets. The temperature had not changed much, but the loss of the wind made it seem as if he had stepped into an oven.

Delbert glanced around and saw they were in an enclosed grotto. Behind them was a hulking, ornate building that could be a temple. The facework of the building seemed to be of marbled stone, while the floors had the appearance of modern terrazzo. The other three sides of the grotto were masonry buildings with long porches of heavy, red-stained wood.

A mousy, gray-haired man ran up with three robes. "I am Bob Hostig, senior resident for Dustin-Rhodes, Virdea."

The Big Man shook his hand. "Is our opposite number already here?"

"They are here. We have installed them in the conference room. Please put these robes on; it is protocol."

Bob Hostig had huge recessed eyes, set into a head too large for his tiny body. Delbert almost asked him whether he was human but refrained. It was unlikely he had ever had a visit from three of the most powerful people in the company, and he seemed completely unable to master the protocol. He bowed and scrapped, used lots of sirs, and despite the temperature of the grotto, he was repeatedly wiping sweat from his shiny pate.

The robes turned out to be unisex taffeta sarongs, long lengths of gold-colored, shiny-slick cloth, designed to be wrapped around the body. Delbert was not sure what protocol called for wearing the strange clothing, but he was willing to go along since The Big Man seemed unfazed by the request. Hostig led them into a side building and took first their cold weather gear, followed by their street clothing, then left to allow them to tie their own sarongs.

The Big Man immediately tied his sarong like a muumuu, leaving his shoulders bare, while the Executive Vice President created a terrible floppy mess that showed off his boxer shorts. Delbert kept his pants on and simply tied a double shoulder wrap, allowing his machine gun and pistol to dangle, exposed. The lack of instructions said that tying the sarong your own way might be part of the protocol.

When they dressed, a dark-skinned man in a suit of chain and an elaborate feathered headpiece entered, carrying an odd three-piece crossbow. It was cocked by holding the center shaft and throwing the weapon forward like the motion used to open a balisong knife. It probably threw bolts with less force than an arbalest, but it seemed like it was faster to shoot. He was met in a hallway by a woman with an elaborate face tattoo and laminar armor like a Japanese knight, holding a spike ball-and-chain thrown over her shoulder. The man with the crossbow wore the crossed "D and R" of the Dustin-Rhodes Corporation, while the tattooed woman had a symbol of a modern interpretation of a human brain tilting as if under acceleration. Two more guards, one from each company, joined them halfway down the hall, and a third set at the end. The first set entered the conference room, followed by The Big Man, the Executive Vice President, and two more guards. The final two guards were posted at the door. Delbert looked around the alcove and saw a tea set by which stood a beautiful oriental woman with shocking blond hair.

"Care for a tea, mate?" she asked. Her accent was a brittle but fascinating Australian brogue.

There was no reason an Asian woman should not have an Australian accent. He looked her up and down. She had an unusual Armalite rifle slung on her back and a blocky automatic on her right hip. The modern weapons said this was his opposite number; the only ones allowed such arms. "Please, cobber."

"Cobber, is it?" She poured water on matcha powder without any attempt at ceremony then split her cup into two. He nodded at her caution and took his cup. He tasted the tea. It was bitter as if someone had made espresso and used the left-over grounds for a second go. "Disgusting."

"I agree, too much tannin. Enough caffeine to kick a bull in the balls, though."

Delbert nodded. "Delbert Devine," he said.

"Name's Cleary McCabe, you want to work this out?"

"Might as well."

They walked together down the hall to a solarium. Some Monks in purple taffeta scattered like geese when they entered the room, leaving them alone. McCabe sat down on a chaise and motioned him to an opposite one. They were frugal rosewood racks like bath furniture instead of overstuffed monstrosities. A jute mat was the only attempt at providing comfort. The solarium, though, had huge windows with two layers of real glass set into one-foot panes, allowing the sun to warm the room. The glass was not good enough to allow the visitor to see the outside, but it was better than nothing. Delbert sat down. "May I call you Cleary?"

"Of course. And you are Delbert?"

"By preference. My entire name makes me sound like a tent evangelist." He sipped his tea and said, "Desired bottom line."

"The Doctor returned FOB New York City, 2020, into the custody of the agents of Brain Trust Corporation."

"Kidnap or voluntary?"

"Maximum deference to her wishes; however, if it comes down to it, she must be held at any temporal location and made available for a few hours to the CEO of Brain Trust, lacking a more suitable solution."

Delbert nodded at McCabe "Now give me the downsides. The more you tell, the better it is for me."

She looked him in the eyes and said, "Dr. Brainerd is the CEO's daughter, estranged. He has had a heart change resulting from recent events of a health-related manner and wanted to make amends."

"How estranged?" Delbert asked.

McCabe said, "From the point-of-view of the daughter, very much so."

"With justification?" He looked at her odd rifle, made of plastic and black metal. A space rifle.

"Mate, I wish I knew." McCabe stared at the panes of blurry glass. "What is your plan?"

Delbert said, "Far as I know, she is with two of my best operatives. I will send three more to track them. The 'Science Joes' think they have a rough landing spot for the group based on where and how they left."

"May I contribute one of my people?" She did not make that sound like a request.

He replied, "By all means. Shooter?"

She shook her head no. "Special Talents. A wizard."

"For fuck's sake." Delbert hated special talents … and hated wizards even more.

McCabe laughed. "Yes, tricky bastards to make a contract with. Real Polly Mollies, if you know what I mean. How about I give you my best shooter as well."

"That would be fine." Delbert considered it. "Any advice on dealing with the Wizard?"

She leaned back in her chair and stared at Delbert. "Stay out his way, but if he gives you too much shit, one behind the ear, and I won't kick. "

Delbert nodded. The power brokers would be at it for hours, but he had work he could do here to be ready when the deal had been hammered out.

McCabe sighed, "The world is problematic when it hands you a trilogy."

Delbert did not know what she meant.

BECALMED IN THE LAND OF REGRET

DATE: 24TH DAY OF THE BEAR, 3684
LOCATION: GREEN SPRINGS, OVERLAND PASS, VIRDEA

Kelle got up when a spray of orange sunshine struck her face, just as she had each day for the past week. Or was it two weeks? It had been long enough that she expected sunshine through the window, the sound of turtle doves in the eaves, a commotion in the courtyard as the early chores were done. She could hear the well pump being pressed and water gushing into wooden buckets as happened each morning. Two ravens were perched above her in the rafters, but they were asleep. It had been a long time since she had seen a raven awake and hopping around.

She worried herself from her encasing blankets and stood up from her bed. She was wearing a soft gown of blue crepe with matelassé trimming, home-made and scratchy warm. As happened every night, a new dressing gown appeared along with new day clothing and an evening dress. Today a funny and warm-looking dressing gown of particolored madras hung by her bed, while a beautiful green organdy blouse and a pleated white batiste-weave skirt were laid on a dresser. Hanging on the closet door was a beautiful brocaded dress in blue with a gray shawl. It was like some parent put out the clothing.

The clothing was simpler than was her normal taste, plain folk style with the hint of homemade, but she fell into them each day with the joy of a girl putting on her first prom dress. Somehow, they always fit her perfectly. It was amazing; normally if tried to wear anything store bought it was a struggle to match her measurements. Either she had to buy from the children's section and put up with the clothing being restrictive around her chest, or she had to buy clothing that assumed she had about five more centimeters of leg than she was blessed with. The clothing here, though, fit perfectly every time.

She put on the morning clothing, took her wooden bathing kit from her pack, grabbed her iPhone and the solar charger she had for it, and then wrapped the day clothing up. At the door of her room, she met a white and black seal point Ragdoll named Chrissy, hair crackling as if it had been brushed out for hours by a loving parent. The cat regarded Kelle with deep blue eyes, yawned, and languidly levered herself to her feet. "Yeow," she said.

"Yeow, yourself," Kelle replied. No matter when she woke, the beautiful cat greeted Kelle at the door for the morning routine. Her first task was to brush the door with her head, then she was responsible for walking between Kelle's legs, touching them with soft bumps and a fierce purr. After Kelle was up and moving, she walked into the vestibus where she stopped and looked over her shoulder, violet and blue piercing eyes beckoning Kelle forward. "Bath time?" Kelle asked.

"Yeow." It replied to any inquiry with the same answer.

The cat was enchanting and wrong. The scientific back of Kelle's mind wondered at the sophistication needed to train a cat to perform the small tasks this one did. There was magic, of course, but how far did magic go?

So she followed the beautiful little cat's slinky progress. Her own sleeping quarters were a little out-building with its own fireplace, chimney, and stack of firewood. The firewood was always restocked in the morning from the night before, and she had never discovered who cut it, another fact that niggled at her intellectual mind. Two other small buildings, a workshop, and another guest house formed a compound with the main house, a compact red painted structure with a giant porch.

As she followed her cat-guide, Kelle noticed that the Chevy was being washed by the homesteader M'Qeuen Jks while the mistress El'Lene Jks sat on her porch peeling vegetables. The purple intelligence was quiet, as if constant care and attention was all that was needed to send the ancient spirit back into hibernation. A giant cat, maybe 10 kilos, sat between them on a cushion chair, legs outstretched and front paws on the chair arm like a human. Two more cats hunted the undergrowth of Live Oakes that rimmed the trail back to the Yellow King's Road. Dozens of ravens hung in the trees silently, heads bowed into their plumage like their batteries had been plucked by an impish fey.

The trail Kelle followed wound up the hill behind the compound. On the first switchback, she saw Rains-a-Lot and one of the homesteader's blond kids searching for something in the understory of the trees. He was always teaching the household children or some of the mysterious neighbors something. Woodcraft would alternate with stories of Greek heroes told in a way that Kelle could almost believe the normally taciturn Native American had read them in classical Greek.

She kept walking without alerting them to her presence and then came to a small overlook. Above her, a little waterfall cascaded down from the hills, crashing into a tiny pool, which then streamed forth as a gushing brook. Hundreds of ravens shared the trees in silence, but this was not as noticeable because she could hear screeching red-wing blackbirds, scolding blue jays, and the coo of turtle doves forming an orchestra of sound.

Kelle stopped, and not for the first time, she wondered at the water. It seemed to flow into the valley both from the river and from the falls, but nowhere did it empty from the valley. The unexplained should be outraging Kelle, causing her to seek answers, but instead, the ennui was so deep in her she could both identify its existence and not really care at the same time.

Only, deep inside of her, she knew she cared. She cared and was troubled.

About 200 meters away downstream the path continued to an area littered with rocks where barrels had been upended. She saw Ivy standing among the rocks, nude except for crazy combat boots, his body covered in a fitful lather. He was not cut like a modern American male who powerlifted weights. Instead, he was spare, like a hard life had robbed him of the roundness that civilians saw as normal. His calf muscles were immense, but if he had been a weightlifter, he would have made sure his thighs were proportionally larger. What was notable was his back and chest. They bore the scars of someone who had carelessly allowed their physical self to be challenged by steel, vine, and rock. He was a man who had lived hard, and Kelle was realizing he was beautiful.

Ivy turned, and Kelle smiled, viewing him from the front. Men were so proud of their packages, but to Kelle they just looked silly, dangling about and probably getting in the way of everything. From the front though, she saw Ivy was equally spare, with whipcord muscles and the same pattern of scars that told of a life lived hard. He was not tan like a beach boy, but he had the selective "farmer's tan" of someone whose life was spent in some type of uniform.

It was really when he began to sing that Kelle became enchanted.

Le bon roi Dagobert

Mangeait en glouton du dessert

Le grand saint Eloi lui dit:

"O mon roi vous êtes gourmand

Ne mangez pas tant"

"C'est vrai, lui dit le roi,

Je ne le suis pas tant que toi"

He sang in no particular key but with gusto, and he ended his song by pouring water from the barrels across himself. He then began to dress in plain homespuns, looking like some medieval peasant, except last of all, he put his pistol in its Miami Vice shoulder holster. When he started up the trail, she nodded to her guide cat and started down, so she could pass by as if she had just arrived. "Is that a good place to bathe?"

Ivy said, "Yes. Moreso with those ravens. It was strange to have them all looking at me silently, but I figure they are better guards than even Rains-a-Lot would be. More eyes."

"And more beaks," she replied. She walked down the trail with her Ragdoll partner until she reached the little bathing area. It was close enough to the falls to hear the crashing water but far enough away that it would not pollute the stream. The cat jumped up on a rock and made a soft meow sound. Normally, she bathed in the stream crook, about 30 meters past this point, but the sunlight here was warmer, even if she was more exposed to view.

Kelle shook off the sense of foreboding that was trying to invade her this morning. Instead, she threw her senses out and discovered she was being watched. At first, she thought it was the Ravens, but after a second thought, she knew it was Ivy, and it was a different sort of voyeurism than she was used to. It was not the "crazy stalker watching" that she used to put up with from Judius, the Wizard fuck who was chasing her now, but instead it was an almost endearing combination of protectiveness and desire in conflict. She had not known he was even interested in girls until now. The attention she felt was momentary. He did not stay in his hiding spot, but it was enough to give her a moment of chills.

Once she had washed, she gathered her supplies and started back up the trail. As she walked, she passed Rains-a-Lot speaking to a group of men in the mists of the woods. She looked at them as she walked along until another voice startled her. It was the Troubadour reciting a poem from the comfort of his hammock.

For eye equals one to one thousand,
and pauses quivering for rodent down,
to step aside with screams of next eye! Next eye!
and brilliant clear screen, and stacks built tall and sound.

Reset eye, the mouse does place the easy bet,
you will need all variables again it seems for future dreams,
as the cautious counter sends the pile of numbers around,
first one, then two, to twenty-two thousand and ten.

Back to home, the mouse runs fast as light,
dancing across the count of time set first to last right,
as stack is pointed at towering stack summed high,
and truth pours forth into darting sighted eye.

Then quick as a crazy winking link,
the universe fills with four zeros and two effs in a blink,
the mouse does freeze in its convoluted crazy tracks,
complaining that irrational number twice told has all to seize.

She approached the young man in his luxuriance and warmed her hands by the fire he had lit. "Your poem has some nice rhymes."

He smiled his impish grin. "Shanties need not rhyme."

"Is that so?" Kelle responded.

He smiled and recited again:

Cows tipping summer breeze,
we step along as lovers sneeze.

His voice was filled with wistful abandon. Kelle said, "That one rhymes as well."

The Troubadour replied, "Is that so?" He then looked to the sky and said:

No time to waste, no time to linger,
look out asshole, here comes a finger.

Troubadour laughed. "My psychologist taught me that one."

Kelle smiled, "Not your proctologist?"

The Troubadour considered for a second. "Which one deals with assholes?"

Kelle shrugged. "Both, I guess."

"Yes." He swung up from his hammock. "How is your day?"

Kelle shrugged. "Same as yesterday. Paradise. It is very restful."

"It is that," he said.

There was silence for a minute. Kelle broke it by saying, "I am troubled, Troubadour."

The impish smile crossed his face. He brushed his hair from his forehead and then stretched his arms out. "About what?"

She gestured around at the beautiful glade they were sitting in. "This is all too neat. Have you thought of where the cotton comes from?"

"I am not sure I follow," he said.

"Every day, a new cotton dress shows up in my bedroom. Where is the cotton grown? Who gins it? Who spins it? Could it be the ethereal neighbors who inhabited the verges? Certainly not the Jks family; they never leave their porch."

The Troubadour considered this. "How can you use logic to deconstruct a place like this?"

Kelle felt her muscles tense. "It is through logic that it is possible to deconstruct a place like this." She looked at the Troubadour. He was a beautiful man with a strong face and a sense of sexuality that pervaded his every movement, like he was on stage every second of the day. She had seen frictions between their guide and the quiet, competent Rains-a-Lot and the skilled, calculating Ivy. He tended to be showy and flippant, whereas her protectors were like paladins, quiet, powerful, and if anything, understated.

The Troubadour sat up. "Oh lady, why not indulge in this respite? I have often wanted to find a place and a time where I could just be me, to tell the story of just myself."

Kelle considered this. "What is your story, Troubadour?"

He shook his head. "I do not know. Like you, I was Earth born. Like you, I have wandered this land. Unlike you though, I am drawn back to Earth. Drawn back by gold I wish I did not want so badly to claim."

"What gold is that?" Kelle asked.

The Troubadour looked around as if guilty of some great crime. "Fame. You see, I played the court of the Queen of Fire and Ice and was spirit marked for it. And I know

I have the magic to make people listen to me. I think the Queen has that intention for me. She sent me back to Earth."

Kelle considered this. "When did she do this?"

The Troubadour said, "Years ago … and in the future. You should know Virdea does not have the same connection to linear time for Earthlings as its own citizens."

"If the Queen sent you to Earth, why are you here?" Kelle asked.

"Delaying my return," the Troubadour answered cryptically.

Kelle thought it over. "You should leave Troubadour. Before this place becalms you as well as us."

He nodded. "What of you?"

She smiled at him. "I sense that none of us want to give up a safe land, but I fear we must leave. The perfect place to rest is also a trap."

The Troubadour fell into his hammock and started a new poem, and Kelle followed her guide cat up the trail.

At the compound, she saw the master and the mistress of the house working amid their cats. The sound of birds filled the air, but the Troubadour was onto something. The ravens were notably silent. Kelle found herself a clear space on the large, outdoor table and said, "Another day of wonderful hospitality."

The Master said, "Let me fetch you some lunch."

The Mistress El'Lene then came and sat by her. "I have a gift for you," she said.

Kelle said, "We cannot accept anything else, really, you have been wonderful."

"Nonsense." She pulled from a sisal bag two objects wrapped in jenny-spun haircloth. The cloth was tied up with strings of jute that formed an intricate bow.

Kelle took the packages and opened them both. Inside were two calf-boots with brown canvas uppers and burgundy-red leather lowers. Along the left side of the boots were cleaver buckles that, when released, allowed them to be put on or taken off rapidly. Brass rivets held the lacing in place, and the soles were hobnailed like an old man's work boot. She squeaked in joy, a sound she hated normally when she made it but one that was impossible to suppress, and put them on. They fit like a glove, hugging her feet with a firm yet gentle embrace.

"You look like a person who likes to run," Mistress El'Lene said.

Kelle replied, "I hate running, especially in boots, but these feel great. Can I try them out for a bit?"

Mistress El'Lene replied, "Of course, they are yours."

Kelle got up and ran around the compound like a girl practicing for soccer. It was like the boots knew her feet already. She felt she could run faster in them than soccer shoes, but she also felt they reduced her natural clumsiness a lot. They were literally the most comfortable pair of shoes she had ever worn, which was saying a lot considering they were boots.

Then, she stopped. The problem Kelle had with paradise was that it did not work her intellectual muscles sufficiently. Things here made a certain categorical and even an ordinal sense, but the explanations always broke down in the rational. Each thing she wanted was almost always provided to her. Almost, in that her fashion sense and desires were being short-circuited by some sense of romance and calm. She wanted Ivy. She was an adult woman with a desire to have men in her bed and inside of her. She had, in recent years, started down a path where she was master of her own sex life. So why did she peer daily at the nude form of Ivy and lust after him? Why not walk down to the river as he washed and take him?

She walked down to a working area where Ivy sat, playing with some wood that looked to be parts of a small jewelry box. He looked up at her and smiled.

"We are becalmed," she said.

He sat up, losing his smile. "What do you mean?"

She reached up and touched Ivy's cheek. "This is a trap, dear Ivy, all logic says it is, and we must fight the trap with all of our might."

"I do not sense a trap!" Nonetheless, he had pulled his Browning and was brass checking it.

She watched him work with his weapon, wooden box forgotten on the ground. It made her feel somewhat sad. "Not every trap has steel teeth. Tell me you sense it also. This place is not designed for us. We cannot stay here."

He stopped, holding his pistol in his hands. "The ravens?"

"They have been helping us forward. Why did they go silent?" She waved her hand around her. "We were pressed and found sanctuary. We were tired and found relief. We were hungry and found substance. The only thing we did not find was an end to our quest. This feels wrong.

She watched Ivy react to this chain of thought. "I have parents."

"And Rains-a-Lot has children, and I have a calm place to think, but despite being surrounded by oddities, I do not think original thoughts, and none of the children of Rains-a-Lot are truly his. You sit here building a box of wood and do not gather yourself up, since when is that you?" Kelle turned and saw Rains-a-Lot had entered the clearing. His face was neutral, but his shoulders said he had heard and understood what was being said.

Ivy said, "Why are we heading to the palace of the Queen of Fire and Ice?"

Rains-a-Lot said, "It is a path, any path, through this confusing land." He placed his hand on Rains-a-Lot's for no other reason Kelle could see than animal comfort.

"Does this make the homesteaders our enemies?" Ivy asked.

Kelle shook her head. "This is a magical place. A place of succor. I do not think the masters of this place are evil. I think this place is like a drug."

There was silence among the three for a minute. Then Kelle said, "Our quest is one of empowerment and self-definition. There is nothing silly about escaping evil, or fleeing to a place we hope is better. We are not some whiney story from Redbook. Instead, we are searching for ourselves in a world where people would claim to capture and control us. My father chases me. My former partner chases me. We flee ourselves."

There was silence as she glanced around. She stood up and led the three to where the Chevy sat, walking slowly through the sun-fading woods, listening to the homey and expected tongues of the forest, the wind through the trees, the scamper of small creatures, and the sounds of birds on the wind.

It was almost dinnertime when they reached the homestead, and the farmsteaders were loading the table for another feast. Josey and Rascal, two of the steading cats, sat at the head of the table, while Rains-a-Lot and Ivy had already taken seats and were taking plates of turkey meat from the mistress. The creases in Rains-a-Lot's face were slowly clearing, and he smiled occasionally when he thought no one was looking. For Ivy, the hunted look of a man always on edge had been replaced by the simple demeanor of a person whose concerns were only about the farmlands around the stead. Neither of the men even pretended to keep weapons about their person anymore. Only the ravens seemed disturbed, their peroneus muscles seeming almost unable to hold their mass. She felt the intrusion of the purple thoughts that were from the ancient mind of Mamma LeDeoux. <*You plan to leave.*>

Kelle thought, <*Yes, I do. Will each of you come with me?*>

<*You are the leader, why do you assume anyone will not?*> the 1957 Chevy replied.

<*Why do you say this?*> Kelle asked.

<*Because it is true,*> came the purple thought.

It was a soundless conversation at the edge of a glade, resonating through her body. <*And what does the mother say, Violet?*>

<*Nests are temporary structures built to protect for a time, but there comes a time when health demands that children fly.*>

Kelle pulled down on her sweater to cover her tummy, adjusted the clips that held her short black hair in order, and squared her shoulders. Then, she walked out to the meal. M'Qeuen Jks stood and said, "We have a great meal for you, my daughter!"

Kelle said, "Thank you, but I have used too much of your kindness. I have to leave you now.

El'Lene also stood. "Just a few days, my darling. You must rest!"

"You are too kind, but no. I cannot make my friends leave, but I have a quest to complete."

M'Qeuen added, "You do not understand. As long as you are here, you are protected."

Kelle nodded. "This will still be true when I return."

"You cannot again enter the Green Fields in your lifetime," El'Lene said.

She could sense their sadness, but she had to continue. "I understand, and this saddens me. You have helped us so much, allowed us time to heal in safety. Still, it is time I left."

El'Lene collapsed and sobbed. "Years ago, our son left for the wars. He never found his way back. Now all we get is the ravens, and they are little replacement for our loss. Stay here and let us care for you. This is not sinister, just correct."

Kelle turned away. "I will always remember you and your kind cats. This is a timeless paradise you have crafted. And maybe your son will someday return to live with you." Kelle turned to Ivy who sat silently, staring at his plate of food. "It was kind of you to carry me this far, Mr. d'Seille." She then stepped up to Rains-a-Lot and hugged him. "You will each be my friends forever."

She turned and did not look back. On the trail, she met two cats, Rascal and Josey. Josey's slick black fur shined in the growing moonlight of the second moon, while Racal was visible simply because of his great size. "Is this rebellion, Master and Mistress Catus?" she asked. Behind her, she heard the soft approach of the Chevy. She turned and saw the farmsteaders standing stoically as Rains-a-Lot and Ivy walked by the side of the Chevy, which was being driven by the Troubadour. She touched her heart and lips, and she lifted her hand to the sky. From her fingers, a star of light launched into the sky. She turned to Rascal and Josey and said, "That star will bring their son back to them, someday, I hope."

Josey turned and walked into the woods, but Rascal seemed to consider the gift, then walked up to her and bumped Kelle's knees with his forehead. Then, he also turned and walked into the woods.

THE DEAD IN THE SNOW

DATE: NOVEMBER 30, 1890
LOCATION: YANKTON, SOUTH DAKOTA

It was 14 years after his adoption, and the wild orphan named first Rains-a-Lot, and then Cry-Baby, had grown into a man under the tutelage of his gentle parents, the Quakers, and schools where Native Americans could learn to be almost as good as whites. Marlow Smith had died the year before, and his foster mother had looked at her foster son, the only child she could claim living in this world, as her pride. And now her pride was out in the world, fulfilling a promise he had made to himself years ago.

Jim Smith, attorney-at-law, sat in the rocking train car as it sped across the landscape at 30 mph or more. He was a lawyer thanks to his passing two years of rigorous schooling at Drake University, gaining an acceptable score on the Iowa Bar, which permitted Indians and women "of good character" to take the test (but failed to designate that status for white men), and several years of work at a Chicago law firm.

He checked his watch. It was a gold-colored brass pocket model manufactured in 1889 by the American Watch Company, and it was sold from an Indian Territory agency store to Blue Flower, his adopted mother. It was a good watch, and Jim was proud of it. Its presence in his pocket said that Indians could learn. Some of his Cherokee friends, despite a hundred years of contact with whites, saw a simple pocket watch as a magical being who could take charge of a person's life. For Jim, it was just a tool that aided him in catching a train on time.

In keeping with the weather and Jim's social class, he wore full-length tweed trousers, a Norfolk jacket in tasteful green and, in recognition of his role as a lawyer, a carefully tied crepe four-in-hand, topped off by a full-sized velvet topper, all of which he had purchased from Arleigh Phelps Gentleman's Outfitters. His steamer, of course, held a very modern tuxedo that young lawyers were making popular in the best restaurants, while he kept a levée coat for court. His fellow law students said Jim could almost pass as white, and all of them agreed that if Grant was willing to put up with Ely S. Parker, then the fashionable man on the make needed at least one Indian in their circle. Hell, they exclaimed, the rumor was Parker married a stunning white woman 20 years his junior.

The sound of the train was hypnotic. Its precision was astounding. According to his watch, in 17 minutes, the train would pull into Yankton and deliver him with 4 hours to spare for his court appointment with the Federal District Court of South Dakota, said state having just celebrated its first birthday a few weeks back. It was no wonder that the simple pocket watch was seen as magical by some Indians. With one, the world could be yours. Without one, you were at best late.

As predicted, the train pulled into the station on time. The court meeting, though, was postponed. Jim stood in the judge's office while the portly man tried to explain.

"This whole Ghost Dance thing has people scared. The thinking is, if there is any court interference, it should wait for the courts to finish their move to Sioux Falls. Shoot fire son, how old were you when Custer got himself bushwhacked?"

"Fifteen, Your Honor." Charging 500 men into the maw of 20,000, expecting pluck and luck to save you, was hardly being bushwhacked. The modern theory though was that Custer was ill-used by the Indians who for some reason resisted the massacre of their women and children or their starvation on ill-suited reservations. Nothing had really changed since then. The young lawyer looked at the older one and noted the man actually might be scared of Indian attack, as absurd as that may seem. He was fidgeting with nerves and had wisps of hair sticking out from his court cap.

"Then, you remember how scared folk were. Getting scalped is no Sunday lark." The judge looked out the window with a crease between his eyes. Did Jim sense the ghosts of the plains warriors this man had hung slowly gaining power in his heart? Could the Ghost Dance be working?

Jim's memory of it was distinct. His name then was Rains-a-Lot, and he was 15 summers old. With a reckless desire for glory, he had ridden down the blue coats and leapt from his horse onto a dismounted officer who held the name Thomas Custer. The man shoved his pistol into Jim's chest, but it had no ammunition. Jim swept it away with his coup stick, then struck the man on the head. He then pulled his knife, a huge blue Bowie made by a cutler in Prairie City, and carved away the soldier's scalp who screamed and tried to claw it back into place. His yell raised to an ululation as Jim/Rains-a-Lot/Cry-Baby buried his knife into the man's chest and cut the man's heart. He held up the beating organ for his friends and brothers to see, then bit a big chunk of it out and spit it onto the dead man's chest. As the judge so ignorantly said before, *"Getting scalped was no Sunday lark."* It was a horrible, terrifying, painful, and usually final act to a life of amazing experiences. It was a denouement that no reader could understand unless the book they were reading was equipped with scything blades to cut off their hands at the last chapter leaving their eyes to watch as the novel they held devoured their flesh in great gobs. When Ivy had scalped someone, he had lacked the words to describe it and had been left crying for weeks. Now, the words were like icicles that formed across the ethical armor the Quakers had tried to fix to his soul.

The judge lit a cigar but did not offer one to Jim. "Boy, give this one a rest. Those Indians will shout it out, and then they will be back to the reservation." He picked up a bottle of Calvados and considered it. Two preserved apples floated in the liqueur.

Jim said, "They do not have enough to eat." He picked at his collar, stiff and starched. A white man's collar.

The portly judge looked up from the bottle of imported brandy. "Then, they should plant crops. Hell, whites starve also, more than they probably suspect. You don't see a starving white farmer leaving their farms and declaring war on their government."

"Have you seen the land they have been given?" Jim almost said, "My people." He was tolerated because he was a "Cherokee" who was rumored to be half-white. If they ever discovered he was born on the far side of this new state in a leather hut to a warrior and his wife, or that he had killed the brother of the yellow hair and eaten his heart, then his role in the court system would be decidedly different. If he had been a white criminal with some personality, he would be forgiven, then shot in the back like they shot Wild Bill Hickok. He was an Indian, so he would simply be declared hostile and killed.

Despite this, underneath his coat was a reminder of whom he was. On a Murphy leather shoulder holster was Thomas Custer's very own Schofield Smith & Wesson Model 3 revolver. He carried it everywhere but had never used it since the fight at Little Bighorn except to shoot cans from fence rails.

The judge dismissed him from the chambers. Outside of the courthouse, Jim stood and wondered what to do. He was still considering this when a man, an Indian with the vision of the plains radiating from his being, appeared. "You talk, and they not listen."

"You could say that."

"Your mouth not made for talk."

"Then what in the Father's name is it made for?" Jim was angry and taking it out on this poor wretch, standing on the steps of a courthouse that was not long for this world, in a city whose meaning was ending.

"It was meant to bite power, to turn the soul power of the white man against them. It was you who ate the Custer heart and stole all that power, only to disappear into the plains."

Jim pulled the man aside. He was frail and old, looking more like a person who caged drinks from bar patrons by telling their fortune than a truth-seer of the Lakota. Yet, how could he know what no one living did? The cold metal of Custer's revolver throbbed under his heavy coat.

"The whites, they find the brother of Custer. They see he is scalped, his chest torn open and his heart removed, and they hear the stories. Your name in English is not Rainmaker, no?"

"Rains-a-Lot."

The old Indian said, "So the whites, they ask which Indian did this to the brother of the yellow hair. And people whose mouths should not speak say it was Rains-a-Lot. Only whites, when do they ever hear what is said? It is *Ité Omáǧau* they say, Rains-in-the-Face, he is who did these things, and Rains-a-Lot, the true author, disappears into the grass and into memory."

Jim Smith, who was Rains-a-Lot to the Lakota or *a-tlo-yi-hv a-yo-li,* "The Crying Child" to the Cherokee, had many names. But this old man knew the one in which his crimes were committed. The preachers at his mother's home said killing was wrong, an unforgivable sin. He preferred his sins not be said out loud so that the God of the Christians would not hear he was responsible. "This was long ago."

"This was not long ago. This was yesterday and tomorrow. I was sent to find the man for whom time does not exist, the person who could mold the power of the Ghost Dance into a weapon, which would send the white man fleeing on their iron beasts to behind the sunset and would open the graves of those who have died these many years for a new time of plenty. Is it a coincidence that the place I was told to find the man, at the time it was said he would be present, you who ate the heart of Thomas Custer should appear before me, showing the aura of both Eagle and Bear just days before the dance brings forth its milk to feed the lands?"

Jim fell into the face of the old man, the thousands of crags that covered it like a topographic map of his soul, each one telling of a day of wind, of rain, of sun, or of freezing snow. He saw the pocks of disease that struck young and the shrunken cheeks that told of limited food. He saw the three ritual scars that a tribal elder placed on his cheeks seeking wisdom, and the scar on his forehead said he had fought as a younger man for the heart of a woman. He saw woven in his hair an eagle's feather, and around his neck hung 11 bear claws. He saw a dab of red paint that proclaimed purpose and the slight yellow that spoke of a life quest.

The old man braced him. "Last night, I had a dream, and it was of you. I saw you riding a steed of iron through a great magical tornado. I then saw you walk among strangers yet know you were one of them. I saw you step forward to proclaim your mastery, leading a thousand dancers in a dance that heals a great rift. I see you holding the worthy dead and your touch brings them to life. I see you an old man with many children, and they all call you the Rainmaker. They will say you saved your people, though they did not know you as theirs."

Jim stared into the man's eyes. They were black pools of understanding, tinged with memory and pain and fear and all the other emotions that being born on the plains brought. The man stepped back from his embrace and held out his hand. "Come with me to the Ghost Dance, help me rescue our kith, and bring forth a new world."

They could not know that the winter would turn, and the dancers would die in the snow.

WARSONG FOR A FRAGILE QUEEN

DATE: 3RD DAY OF THE POSSUM, 3651
LOCATION: THE BANYON PALACE, EMERALD CITY, VIRDEA

The mirror represented freedom to Warsong. He had complained to the Queen about being a captive in the beautiful palace, and she had surprisingly responded by giving him the Mirror of Stepping. The copy of that mirror currently sat in a gentleman's tailor in Manhattan. At any time, Warsong, who was called Randolph in a past life, could step through to the other side and be home. He had not yet.

Sometimes the mirror played tricks. It would show images of men who were dressing in fine suits and admiring the cut of their new clothing purchases. Most of the time, the mirror reflected the room it sat in. Here, the sitting room was a roughly oval space built from the wood of the living banyan tree that made up the bulk of the palace. Long, tall splits in the wooden walls formed regular windows, lacking glass, they carried simple shutters that were only closed for winter storms.

It took him a while to figure it out, but the mirror did not reverse his image, nor did it show his reflection perfectly. Today, he was wearing a brocade court jacket in the Queen's yellow and ice blue colors with his own symbol, a spear crossing a treble clef. In the mirror, though, the treble clef was replaced by the backward “E” of an alto clef. He brushed his hand on his Ramirez. In the mirror, his hand for a second became transparent, with only bones showing. It was as if the Ramirez were an X-Ray.

“Warsong, you must be attentive.”

His tutor was a sage from the University, Doctore Losthace. “Must I?” Warsong replied.

“Your place in court is precarious until you can at least understand who the players are,” Losthace said.

“So who is on first base?” Warsong asked.

Losthace frowned. “I cannot say, but I can tell you of the Kings of Virdea.”

Warsong rolled his eyes. “Then tell me who these kings are.”

“Each of the great city-states has a king who ranks equal to the other kings. There is Bagan-Tell, Carkoza, Nimruii, Monje Dar, Steadfast, and Sur. Each is known by the color of their banners: red, yellow, orange, silver, gold, and blue. Each is also known by their sigil: stag, dragon, hawk, ram, bull, and dolphin. Whose name did you forget last night?” Losthace’s voice was patient, but his eyes were intense.

Warsong sighed. “The man in the yellow armor.”

“Who is no man?” Losthace asked. “He is addressed as His Holy Majestic Entity.”

“Sure,” Warsong replied.

Losthace lectured, “He is Rhackhar Zil by name, and the Yellow King commonly.”

“He was drunk and trying to get into the Queen’s pants,” Warsong said.

Losthace shook his head. “The Queen wears no pants, Warsong.”

“Probably why he failed.” Warsong grinned at the joke that was not getting through.

Losthace sighed. "Today, the Queen meets the Troubadour and wants you by her side. In fact, if you meet this Troubadour early enough, the Queen feels that it will save no end of trouble." The academic paused. "There is something worrying her beyond this. Meeting this Troubadour is important for the Queen."

"That is my duty, meeting people," Warsong stated.

Losthace pushed the book, *Vetisilgilias' Encyclopedia of the Nobles and Heroes of Virdea*, at Warsong. "Keep studying, before some noble presses the Queen as to your, ah, regularity."

Warsong had come from a pleasant upbringing. In the storybooks, it was said that he was born near the great Western Ocean in the land of Calis Forelda, but Calis Forelda was convenient only because it was an island no one could place on a map and no one was from. His guitar was said to be possessed by the spirit of a great musical prodigy, which was true, but the rest of his biography was pure fabrication. The mundane fact was that he was from Earth, and his magical guitar had propelled him here to the court of the Queen of Fire and Ice.

He turned his attention to the person gathering his papers and preparing to leave the room. When Losthace departed, he grabbed up the magical Ramirez and left himself for the levee.

The corridors of the palace were green-brown wood, the natural color of the Great Virdea Banyan. Tree herders formed the interior cavities of the tree into useful spaces by blocking and redirecting the fast-moving tendrils versus using mirrors to persuade heartwood to become exterior bark. Planted above a hot spring like the Green Palace of the Emerald City, the tree remained warm year-round.

The palace was always growing, at least a little bit. The tree herders Warsong talked with referred to the tree as having leading and trailing sides. The leading side was in the process of forming new rooms and corridors. The tree was always being folded in on itself to keep it on a useful path, its corridors resembling a constantly growing spiral, which left the trailing side to constantly be lapped by the leading side. Trailing rooms slowly lost their access to sunlight and thus started to close. Some would be preserved by using cedar wood to create tight walls, but many would exist only a decade or two, starting as new leading rooms, surviving middle age, and then meeting the next generation on its way around the tree.

There was an introspective feeling to the palace. In a land that was ageless and timeless, you could never visit the palace twice and see the same thing. It was like the complicated Queen. Warsong was originally just Randolph, refugee from Earth, but she had called him Warsong after he played for her a little scrap of music he had been writing.

What if I saw tonight,
A life that was filled with delight
Yet in the fallen star there was no more fight,
A fallen warrior who has no right....

He passed a pair of guards dressed in red and blue livery, puffy pants, jerkins of color-dyed leather, and steel helmets shaped to look like fish holding a Banyan tree in their mouths. They were talking to the staff from the Butler's Pantry, their own livery having a crossed fork and knife, lacking the leather war armor. The gaggle bowed slightly as he passed, despite his lack of rank.

"You are pensive," Nightface said. His guitar spoke only to him, and it had been a few months before he could differentiate between it and his own inner voice. He gripped the instrument and played a short refrain.

"Mary Had a Little Lamb"

"Like I said, pensive," Nightface said sternly.

He swung off the looping corridor into the kitchens. They were a brick building connected to the palace by a series of skyways. It was a common joke that when a newcomer asked for the kitchens, the reply was to send them to the leading edge of the spin-ward portion of the palace and tell the inquisitive person to wait there and that the kitchens would be along shortly. They provided a pretty reliable shortcut between the stonework walls and the trailing part of the palace that had yet to fail Warsong. He passed into the traditional building and immediately saw Hablesmith, the senior chef of the Queens Cooking Battalion. The short-bearded man treated his undercooks as soldiers in an army, and each meal was a forlorn hope or a mighty siege. The Dwarrow was round as a pear, and in his whites, he looked like a bearded snowball. He yelled at Warsong, "A song, master musician!"

Warsong played a simple riff over three times to the cheers of the kitchen.

"Song of Autumn"

He bowed as he left, entering the corridor to the three-level levee room. He nodded at guards and courtiers as he took his place near the throne. He was about to address Admiral Gane on the status of the far-flung fleets when a newcomer approached. He was dressed in the clothing of a traveler: blue cotton walking pants, a leather belt with a small sword hanging from it, a loose cotton shirt over an undershirt, both in white, and a leather jacket. His hair formed an undisciplined dirty brown halo around his sharp face. Warsong knew this traveler slightly.

"Jack?" Warsong addressed the man by first name.

"Troubadour, please. You are Warsong?" replied the Troubadour.

Warsong bowed. "Yes."

"We know each other," the Troubadour stated.

"You asked me to join your group," Warsong replied to the statement.

Troubadour considered this. "I did. Did you?"

"I said I would think about it," Warsong answered.

"Time is strange in Virdea. You always have to check the when and where of it," Troubadour stated.

Warsong asked, "You do not bill yourself a musician?"

The Troubadour shook his head. "No, I should probably not do that elsewhere. I am a poet and a storyteller. Music just provides the beat."

"Is that all music does?" Warsong asked.

"Without music, life would be a mistake," the Troubadour responded.

Warsong considered this. "Clever."

The Troubadour smirked. "Not me. I first heard that in a class in St. Petersburg, Florida. It is actually Friedrich Nietzsche."

Warsong considered this traveler. It was the first person from Earth he had met in Virdea. Everyone in Virdea was aware of Earth. The membrane was permeable with people slipping back and forth across the startide gates. He glanced over his shoulder—the Queen was not in the vestry yet. "What brings you to this court?"

The Troubadour said, "For the Queen can send me back to Earth."

"Why would you want that?" Warsong asked.

The Troubadour started to say something but seemed to change his mind. "What do you know of magic?"

Warsong considered this. Magic was a simple thing that defied explanation. Everything was magical in Virdea, at least a little. There were people who treated this as a science; they called it hermantics, the study of the flow of magic. For Warsong, it was just easier to accept it as something different, like flan in Mexico, just a new thing to find on the menu. Some places just did not make flan. "Do not ask the Queen in levee for this boon," he finally stated.

The Troubadour looked confused. "Why not?"

"The Queen is of two minds, always. When she has something to give, she asks why give, and she asks why not give. The court's trolls are jealous of boons, so they try to push her more to say no to strangers. That way, when they present their own requests, she is more apt to say yes."

Warsong waved his hand at the Minder, Jaze Jakobian. Jaze was an older man who always carried a large book chronicling the Queen's court schedule. The Minder was a walking font of information on court process. "Master Jakobian?"

"Master Warsong," Jakobian replied.

"Is it possible to move the Troubadour's session to the interior levee on my behalf?" Warsong requested.

Jakobian replied, "If you place your name as sponsor, then he would be interior levee and would not be presenting now, but this afternoon."

"I would be pleased if you did this, Jakobian."

"It is my pleasure, Warsong."

The Troubadour laughed. "You have the way of this place."

"Not really, I am a tolerated stranger, but I accept it because of how much there is to learn," Warsong said.

The Troubadour looked pensive. "So, on magic."

"Yes," Warsong stated.

"Have you considered its potential on Earth?" the Troubadour again censored himself.

Warsong frowned. "I know that it would be difficult to bring home. It is not like a trip to Mexico where you can bring a T-Shirt back, is it? Magic is this place, not something that can be bottled."

"But what if some aspects of magic could be brought back?" the Troubadour asked.

Warsong considered it. "I do not know how that would work. Have you spoken with someone who knows such things?"

"Not yet. It is unimportant if there is no way back to Earth from Virdea. However, I have learned things. That there is a crack in time," the Troubadour said.

Warsong noticed Jakobian was standing behind them, listening. "Master Jakobian, can you have the Troubadour escorted to the minor presence chamber and have him seated with me for dinner instead of with the lesser visitors?"

"Of course, Master Warsong." The Minder turned and waved down a court officer and relayed the requirements, then he turned to the Troubadour, "Troubadour, you will follow this man?"

The Troubadour bowed. "Of course." He had a half smile on his face, as if this was all a cosmic joke or lines in a story he had no part in writing but found humorous nonetheless.

The Queen was late but likely would not be much later, so after watching the Troubadour walk out of the main presence chamber, Warsong took up his position by Swordsman Shiel and Lady Acorna, her Mistress of Plant of Field. The main reason that Warsong stayed with the Queen's Court was the opportunity to just make music, any sort, and in any way he wanted, without the requirement that he does anything else except for these short court appearances. The court appearances, though, had allowed Warsong a chance to see how a grand dictatorship in a magical world functioned, and it also allowed him to get to know a Queen in a way that most of her subjects could never understand her.

It was only a few minutes before the Queen came out. Her dress was a silk and taffeta brocaded suit, a long sweeping gown of the finest worst, and a head-piece of radiating triangles. Her clothing was obviously magical. She wore little mundane in public, as the red, black, blue, and orange pattern on her dress seemed to shift as she moved as if she were a hole cut in the universe and the pattern was fixed in time and space behind her. She was also affected by an odd aura. Her skin was softer in a levee than in other times, like you were seeing it through a camera lens lightly coated with Vaseline, while behind her burned a slight suggestion of flames.

Levee was a fascinating time because it was an expression of how the Queen pulled off the government in the chaos of Virdea. Each person in her Kingdom was entitled to petition to be heard by her. For every length of 10 days, she held six days of levee, two hours per day. Courtiers from all corners of the kingdom attended these levees, and every choice the Queen made was recorded and made available for public consumption by crier or posted notice.

The courtiers had a role in this. As they listened to what was, in essence, a sales pitch to the Queen, they could signal what they thought of the pitch in several ways. They could politely speak with each other in a low voice, indicating a lack of concern for the subject. They could speak louder, gasping and clinking their teeth, indicating the subject as one that was a vital issue. They could also boo or cheer the petitioner. The Queen could in turn take what the courtiers thought into consideration or occasionally angrily reject it.

The first petitioner was a merchant who wanted tariffs on the South Road lowered. "Kasby, Merchant of the City of Kask, dealer in fine wines," the court crier Ottobeila yelled. She was dressed in an Ice Blue uniform and had the darker skin of a highlander, her hair done in magnificent ringlets. The first three parts were formulaic. The crier had to yell the name of the penitent, their rank and class, and where they were from. The last sentence was wholly the realm of the crier and was usually determined by a small amount of bribery, although here Ottobelia's well-known love of claret could have led to the minor superlative.

The wine merchant approached and bowed at the balk line drawn on the floor. Kask was the only real city in the realm with weather that made it ideal for wine production, and its merchants were wealthy and important members of the business community. The courtiers became quiet, and the Queen crooked her finger, which stood in place of her normal imperious command to "Stand tall and be heard."

"Your majesty, the recent tax on goods traveling the South Road has imposed a double penalty on the wine trade, which must ship grapes from the fields to the market, and then must ship wine by the road to the capital for consumption. This tax is enough to make our goods unable to trade competitively with the wines of Luria and the city-states."

And that was the first key to a successful court argument. By tradition, a petitioner held the floor as long as they wished. By practice, they made their arguments quickly and let the discussion move about the room as it needed to. In this case, the decree that produced the taxes along the South Road was created by a group of smaller ports who wanted a share of the shipping that went through Kask; Kask did not object because its own docks were swollen with trade, and the smaller ports agreed to share port fees with Kask. Faced with a small tax on road transport, luxury goods were not deterred from using Kask, but staples like grain were.

Everyone was happy until now, when the Kask wineries brought forward a complaint. The Queen could rule now, pass it to one of several advisors, or request a private audience. She looked about the room and said, "Master Qouth?"

Master Qouth was a tall, skinny man with hair almost as curly as Warsong's. He not only wore the standard brocade blue and orange jacket of a courtier but also affected a thick iron chain that designated his being tied to the lower social classes. The master of citizens (who ignored his duty to the common people) had a tendency to be hanged by just such a chain from the city gates late in the evening, which was perhaps his most important duty, to act as an escape valve for the steam of the masses.

"The wine trade is important for employment in the Southern tier and is beloved by the people in the delta and metone regions. It is possible an exception can be made for transport of grapes under the theory of end use."

The Queen turned to Statius Sindelis, the puffy-cheeked master of laws and traditions, "Do you concur?"

"There is no legal reason why that exception should not stand scrutiny, Your Majesty," Sindelis said.

"Record my support for the proposal, Master Jakobian," the Queen ordered.

Jakobian had his huge book put onto a pedestal already, and a stack of other books that needed to be modified. A hedge stood between them and cast the short spell, the Jakobian entered the note on the monthly book, after which the pages of the other books rustled and creaked as they received the same notation, magically added to their texts. A flurry of librarians then ran those books out of the room and returned with books needed for the next ruling.

The Queen was a workhorse, and for two mind-numbing hours, every 10 minutes, or so, a new issue was brought to the court's attention. Not every ruling was common sense, beneficial, or even kind. One of the Lurian spies had gained an audience to ask for his freedom and instead was dragged out of the room and beheaded, his dripping ghastly head returned for the court to recognize and enter judgment into the books. More than one penitent was dragged from the room kicking and screaming.

When the levee was over, the Queen said, "Warsong, walk with me to the internal levee." He nodded, falling in at her side while Quicksword and Hammerfoe, her two personal guards, allowed them to pass and took up places behind them.

Her dress froze in a pattern as they left the public room. "Play my song," she commanded.

He began to strum a melody.

The song dragged and echoed through the wooden hallway, finding ways to reverberate and speak back to Warsong. Sometimes the tree would pick up on a song and resonate it from its bark, replying in odd syncopating tunes. And this would attract the smaller fey, cat-like winged creatures that were allowed to run free through the palace because of their fondness for eating voles. A flurry of fey-cats soon were singing to the song, *la-la-la-la-la*. It was during these magical moments that Warsong would begin to hum softly like a breathed-flute.

It was rare enough that the Queen stopped. When she did, the fey-cats lit their thoraxes and began to perform for the Queen, a scintillating dream display of sound that urged Warsong to coordinate with them. They would cluster first to the leading then the trailing side of the Queen's private corridor, and he would follow with sound before taking on a new song.

The impromptu concert drifted down the corridors of the great tree and caused work to stop all around the palace. Guards unlocked their knees and lost their professionally distant vision, while cooks in the deepest pantries stopped sorting potatoes for the next meal. The great tree, witness to so many miracles, could still surprise the worldly staff.

Warsong, transported now, was one with a magical guitar, a giant tree, and dozens of little harmonizing fey-cats. Then, they all returned to the original music, sometimes syncopating out to other tunes, until they finally landed back into the field of silence.

The Queen turned and walked into a well-lit alcove, causing the fey-cats to scatter. Warsong followed.

"The person who visits is from Earth," the Queen stated.

Where did she get her information? Warsong did not speculate. The Queen was saturnine, dark and exotic, with a face that could show anger and joy in a single tableau. "Yes, Your Majesty."

"Earth is ripping itself to pieces," the Queen said.

Warsong nodded. "If your majesty says." Then he added, "The stranger is talking about a crack in time."

"Interesting. And this crack is a point where all could fall into chaos. Your heroes, the ones who could change its direction, die one by one, victims of these weapons in the hands of the evil and the misguided. In Virdea, a hero cannot be felled by a single coward. We struggle forth, protected from the worst of our impulses, though Earth teaches us so much sometimes." The Queen sketched a pensive look on half of her face.

Warsong pressed, "Your Majesty, what can I do to help you ease your concerns about Earth?"

"You can be part of what saves it. The Troubadour, he has much to do before he meets me for the first time. And you have so much to do as well," the Queen said dryly.

There was silence for a minute. Warsong did not completely understand what he was to do.

"You do not see it?" the Queen questioned.

"No, Your Majesty," Warsong replied.

"You have learned magic, through music. The Troubadour has learned magic through performance and poetry. Each of you carries the message of Virdea in your heart. Return to your world and live through the crack in time." She paused her speech for a second then added, "You may not heal this crack in time, but you, I foresee, could aid in its healing."

Warsong bowed. "If you ask this of me, I will."

"Thank you, Warsong." She looked out the window. "We may not meet again."

Warsong looked at the slow-moving river that formed the Least Delta of the Lands of the Dual Monarchy. It would be sad not to see this again, but he had asked for the mirror and the right to return to his own land. He knew it was a possibility that, once he returned to Earth, there would be no chance to return to Virdea. He turned from the Queen. "I will, sadly, miss your levee."

"You will be missed at our levee," she replied as she walked away.

ONE BEHIND THE EAR

DATE: 29TH DAY OF THE BEAR, 3684
LOCATION: COLUMB ABBEY, VIRDEA.

The Wizard would not shut up. Cleary McCabe had ventured that Delbert would need to shoot the Wizard at some point, but that freedom did not comfort him. He needed the Wizard, but at the back of his mind, the permission to execute the sot was egging him on.

His name was Gilligan Smith, and he was the most annoying person on Earth or any other world he visited. Delbert, who valued competence above all other characteristics, was immediately put off by the baboon and his affected, prim model of British aristocracy. He wore a suit of tweed, unsuitable for the red scrubs they were passing through, yellow zipper boots, a deerstalker, and a private school tie. They had acquired horses at the abbey and could have had a buckboard, but Smith claimed to be an excellent seat. He was not. When they arrived at camp, the Wizard was complaining loudly and unable to aid in getting water or picketing the horses.

He could do magic, but there was a certain amount of struggle there also. Any request for a spell resulted in a rather lengthy discussion on balance, hermetics, and the opinions of long-dead masters.

The fact, though, was he could use magic. As they progressed across the countryside, they ran into an information wavefront that confirmed this. The story of four people in a purple automobile was already becoming legend. If only he could communicate with Ivy and Rains-a-Lot, they would know help was on the way and to stop traveling south.

"Virdea is a relatively new name, you understand," Smith said.

"Really?" Delbert's horse was not a comfortable seat. He watched enviously as the two Troubleshooters rode horses like they had taken the seat as children. More than likely, this was their first time atop a horse, and they were each just so competent at anything they did that it gave the illusion of experience.

The Wizard clumsily sawed at the reigns of his horse to stay even with Delbert. "The children's book by L. Frank Baum introduced Virdea as a land far away. There is evidence, though, that he was telling a tale of this land, only sanitized for children."

"Riding through the lowland, you can see how much it looks like Australia. Neverland, Virdea, maybe even Wonderland. But, the stories from these lands are hardly children's fair. They are dark, sometimes horrible tales. Although, interestingly enough, none of the tales are so horrible that humans on Earth cannot offer one that is worse," the Wizard continued.

Fortress and Rodgers checked their horses. Fortress trotted back and said, "Large group ahead. Afraid, sir, they have us scented."

Delbert did not see anything in the rolling terrain. "Any reason to think the worst?"

Fortress was off her horse. She had one of the Company's new-fangled battle rifles in one hand while holding her horse in the other. Rodgers said, "Don't know sir. Does this one know anything useful?"

Gilligan Smith looked angry. "You do not know your place. I have read everything about Virdea there is to read. What experience do you have with Virdea?"

Fortress growled. "Thirteen years with the Richland County Sheriff's Department under Leon Lott."

"So you admit no experience?" Smith asked angrily.

"As you say, sir," Fortress replied.

Delbert considered. He then turned his horse to the Wizard. "Give me your assessment."

The Wizard stepped down off his horse with difficulty, almost falling on his ass. Once dismounted, he sat down with crossed legs and began to chant atonally. After a few minutes, he said, "They are people of the land, Mr. Devine."

"And what does that mean?" Delbert inquired.

The Wizard stated, "Farmers, artisans, herders. Quite a few of them."

Fortress groaned and made a hand gesture at Rodgers. Delbert could understand their frustration. What do you call a large mass of farmers, artisans, herders, and the like traveling as a group across the countryside? Delbert looked up and saw several files of armored men running forward from around the contour of the grasslands.

"You are a shithead, Gilligan." Delbert dismounted his horse and waved for the Wizard to do the same.

The two Troubleshooters looked ready to scrap, but Delbert said, "This is dry. If one of you can get away, take the chance and do what is best." That was the beauty of Troubleshooters, you never had to give them detailed instructions. All you had to do was let them off the leash, and they would seek optimal results without requiring endless instructions.

A second stick of soldiers came from behind them, and soon, the tiny valley they were in was surrounded by armed and armored soldiers. About half of the soldiers carried polearms and wore leather jerkins on which a slash of yellow paint had been splashed. A few had lashed bones to their helmets or otherwise tried to incorporate bones into the motif of their dress. A quarter wore mail with shields and axes, and another quarter wore laminar and carried swords and crossbows. They were not formation fighters, though. They came into a rough position, and sergeants yelled themselves hoarse to get them untangled in places so they would be able to fight in close order. There were no words exchanged, and Delbert was willing to let that continue, at least until someone with obvious authority showed up.

After a few minutes of clanking near silence, a mass of horsemen topped the hill in front of them. At their head was a huge man astride a fearsome warhorse; a ball and chain rested over his shoulder, and his pristine steel-plated armor was adorned with a subtle pattern of bones. Directly behind him was a fey woman that was as small and twisted as he was straight and well-formed. Her mount was a yar-horse, a skeletal, muscular, rare animal bred from the magical horses of Yar Krillum. Behind her, three vulpine men in blue and red fox furs with evil smiles and hardened expressions formed together, followed by 25 mounted warriors on a polyglot of mounts with a range of weapons.

The great warrior looked to the Fox-Men and asked, "News?"

One urged his horse to step him forward. "These are refugees from the highlands with no status or power. They seek who we seek. One of them will be, as we have heard in our travels, called Raven."

The group of four that had been chosen for this mission had a number of things in common. Each one of them was fluent in at least one language of Virdea along with English. Each one of them was conceptually well versed on the concept of traveling to another dimension and had agreed to do so for their work. And each one of them had some basic knowledge of the mythical lands. Delbert could understand the language of the lowlands, although his fluency was proving anything but perfect. He recognized a Yar Horse, but this was simply a random shot in the dark; he could not say much about a fey or why she would be twisted physically as she was, nor if the fox-men were qualified to provide information to this rather impertinent knight. False information at that, assuming he actually understood what was being said.

The Wizard, Gilligan, stepped forward and said, "The men in red and blue greet you and claim to be honored at your presence, Mister Devine."

"Oh, shut up Gilligan. I understand what they said." Switching to his best lowland, Delbert said, "I am afraid none of the news from your Fox is accurate."

The twisted woman walked her horse forward. Her voice sounded like the tinkle of fine crystal. "The Fox Bards are loyal to my Lord Devitu d' Cavallu, the soon-to-be Yellow King."

Looking at the fey, Delbert was struck by the same feeling he got when he visited the Fortingall Yew during the war. *Here,* he thought, *is something immortal, yet it is something that time had damaged and that will not grow youthful again. Instead, you have to respect its aged limbs and malformations as great power hidden in a tiny form.*

Delbert commented, "Your Lord Devitu d' Cavallu should understand the sayings are true. One who believes the propaganda dies at the hand of one who believes only the truth."

The bards began to angrily recriminate and throw insults, but they were cut off.

"Silence," the warrior yelled. "Cutwood, you presume too much. Haso, Maldo, and Frisan, step back and be silent." The man sat tall and solid in the saddle of his giant war-horse, his voice projecting like a canon from his helmet. "You are tracking the mechanical monster and her masters, am I correct?"

Gilligan Smith again stepped out and said, "We are master."

Delbert shouted, "Shut up!" and found himself looking into a mass of crossbows.

"Step over here, Master Wizard," Devitu d' Cavallu growled. "How do you track these people?"

Gilligan proudly marched forward and planted his hands on his hips. "Lord, I am using divining, an ancient magical art, to track the metal in the engine that drives the car. No other metal of the same type exists in that mass in all of the lands of Virdea."

Devitu d' Cavallu turned in his saddle to Cutwood. "Is this true?"

Cutwood stared intensely at Gilligan. "This man is disloyal, a liar, and a sycophant, but this one skill, he possesses. We could continue to track the travelers through the density of rumor, but his way is far better for us. In fact, it is the only way we can beat the head start that Lupufocu and Shibbula have."

"I worry also about Ventus," Cavullu opined.

Cutwood stilled her horse and looked vacant into the sky. Ventus is clouded. His piece is off the board. I do not think that Ventus had collected the reins of the quest for the Yellow Crown. If he does not actively seek it, then he can be considered no more than a memory."

Devitu d' Cavallu countermarched his horse and looked out at the rolling grasslands. He pulled his helmet off and hung it from his saddle. His skin was copper or a little darker, and he looked a bit like Ashok Kumar as he appeared in Achhut Kannya—like the powerful warrior could have had deeper depths if the world had let him. "The way fate draws us," the warrior said, "it chews on us and spits us out. If a year ago you had told me that the peerless Mussiǔdragu would fall to an outlander's knife, I would have ordered you gutted as a liar. If you had told me that Viddigatura and all of his kin would die at Potter's Field where I played as a boy in the youth of Carkoza, or that Rossusangutu would die with his face pressed into a puddle of water, I would have chased your shade into the dark worlds seeking a retraction. It keeps growing, though. I contemplate sending assassins against my blood-bonded war brother Ventus. I hunger to bring my morning star down on the head of my oath lord, Shibbula. And instead of solid iron by my side, I contemplate following the directions of a slattern, a hoar, and three fools."

Delbert suddenly felt light on his feet as Fortress grabbed him. Rodgers was blocking them and firing her rifle. They ran into the rolling hills, and Delbert felt his head ducked down by Fortress's hand. There was yelling, horse screams, and explosions going off. Under her voice, she said, "Come on Rodgers, just a kilometer more."

Now, he was horrified. A crossbow bolt had hit her in the thigh, another protruded from her wrist, and two from her chest. It was the one that had struck her cheek and caught on her shoulder that was the most horrible. She was clutching her rifle with one hand, its bolt open and empty. Delbert said, "Stop."

With hundreds of people giving chase, their yells less than a dozen meters away, Delbert could not abandon a person to whom he owed so much. Fortress seemed to take this up, but instead of stopping, she helped Rodgers sit, then started pulling equipment off of her, rations, water bottles, ammunition magazines, knives, a standard issue Browning pistol, and small tools. All of these items Fortress either stuffed in her own pouch or passed off to Delbert. Delbert tried to complain, but Fortress turned and grabbed his lapel. "Stay silent, Mr. Devine. You have nothing to say here." Fortress turned back to Rodgers and said, "Your letter."

Rodgers clawed at the inside pocket of her charcoal suit. Fortress grabbed the letter and said, "Who?"

Blood poured from Rodger's mouth, and she said, "Serena, daughter." Fortress grabbed Rodger's head and kissed it. Rodgers said, "Thanks, enough. The one-eye-gambit."

Fortress said, "You would have been a good partner."

"I would have."

Fortress took a couple of small plastic orbs from her battledress and pressed them into Rodger's hands, then pulled Delbert away and started to run, ducking so they kept below the level of the grass. A few minutes passed, and three explosions popped back where they had just left. Fortress had them run another hour, then threw herself down by a small creek to rest.

Delbert asked, "What is the one-eye-gambit?"

Fortress was a tall, athletic, black-haired woman. She wore odd pixelated battle dress and black quilted body armor, and she was a mass of pouches and pockets. Although her arms and equipment came from Dustin-Rhodes Corporation, the clothing she wore was almost magical in its advancements. Her buckles did not clink, being made of soft plastic. She carried water not only in canteens, but in a bladder on her back. Her pouches carried boxes of ammunition and secured the heavy, clipped magazines used by her rifle, making her look overloaded with gear.

"There are several stories about the battle of Pons Sublicius in 509 BCE, but a few decades ago someone found an etching that told a true story. There were four generals, and they assembled their men outside the city of Rome to give the city the hours she needed to prepare her defenses. The army was defeated faster than they had expected, though. Knowing that if they lost the army, they lost Rome; the generals started to retreat their forces. At the same time, the enemy knew if some of their men could get into Rome with the army, they could throw open the main gates and the city would be massacred."

"Two generals, Spurius and Titus, hit on a plan. They would position themselves in the middle of the bridge and allow only those soldiers they recognized to cross. The problem with this was that the rest of the army would be slowly slaughtered as a result of the bottleneck. For that reason a grievously wounded soldier, his eye missing and his body wended with cuts, volunteered to be the last man killed. He was passed overhead of the retreating soldiers, and then put onto a small stone section of the bridge. At the same time, the bridge behind him was slowly dismantled."

"Horatio fought off the enemy for hours. Our word 'genius' comes from that sort of thing—doing something amazing or being somewhere an amazing thing happens was called genius, and although he died, Rome went on to be an amazing nation. So now, any sacrifice strategy that requires a little luck but allows most of the playing pieces to get away is called a one-eye-gambit."

Delbert leaned back, despair in his voice. "Unlike Rome though, our mission is lost."

"No, it is not. We lost that idiot wizard, but now we have several hundred people guiding us to our final destination. "

Delbert mourned Rodgers, but he couldn't help but laugh.

OURS POLAIRE

DATE: NOVEMBER 15, 1943
LOCATION: SAINT-ÉTIENNE, GERMAN-OCCUPIED FRANCE

The priest wore workman's blues that were turning purple with blood. Despite the Vichy gunshot through his abdomen, he was lucid, at least as lucid as he ever was. Ivy had knelt by his side as he collapsed, caught between 13 and adulthood, not really understanding he was next in line for the traitor's bullet.

"Irony," the priest's voice caught for a second, choked by blood. He kicked his legs feebly, bringing Ivy's attention to the old shotgun that he had been carrying. The priest cleared his throat. "Irony is the coin of human experience."

The old man was the first person who ever cared about Ivy besides his mother. At the start of the war, she arranged for the disgraced priest to tutor her boy while she protected the rambling family house in Vic Sur Seille using tactics Ivy did not want to think about.

Ivy watched as the old priest bled out from a stomach wound, thinking he was a peculiar type of pedophile. He used to watch young boys with an obvious carnal interest, but he never acted on his fantasy. He claimed his conversion to a priest meant he was no longer able to take such pleasures. He was married to God. Despite this, he had been banned from the confessional and defrocked. Luckily for him, the war had intervened, and this saw to his restoration. The children of the city, aware of his predilections, called him the "polar bear," and used to throw rocks at him when they could get away with it, but the old bear had a nasty cudgel and a hunting shotgun that he hand-loaded with rock salt that he would bring boys to account with.

Ivy was his favorite boy and, perhaps, the only person he truly liked. Maybe he considered Angela a friend, the prostitute he visited on weekends whose boyish appearance and willingly wore sailor outfits and plus fours, but somehow, he shared his learning and wisdom with Ivy.

The day he died, Ivy and the priest were loading a mule with cases of 7.5mm rifle ammunition in boxes disguised as turnip crates. It was a bad idea, Ivy and the priest agreed, but the local head of the resistance needed the ammunition to feed their heterogeneous collection of weapons. It was a risk that two noncombatants could take to aid the men and women who fought.

If the boxes had been lighter, then they could have been carried by one person, like a true box of turnips. If they had been filled with turnips, then the loose 15-round boxes and 75-round belts would not have made odd clanking sounds and alerted the Vichy guard. And if it had been Boris the undertaker instead of Andre the baker's son, then the fat laborer would have been asleep. But it was Andre who heard the clanks and shot the priest in the stomach.

The Vichy guard was running forward, yelling for Ivy to lie down. Instead, he grasped the shotgun and shot the soldier through the head. Ivy thought it was like shooting melons as the man collapsed in silence. Like melons, except two shots were bound to bring the attention of the garrison. Andre was dying just like Michaud the priest.

Ivy grabbed the priest's hand. He looked into the boy's eyes and said, "Do you remember when I read you Refus Absurde? In the confessional?" Ivy nodded, and the dying man grabbed the lapel of his chantry jacket. "You must never forget…" Then, he died without further comment.

It was November of 1928 that Ivy was born, brought into the world by a midwife in his mother's family home at Vic Sur Seille. His father had died trying to climb Nanga Parbat just three weeks before, his body becoming one of the dozens that forever inhabited that forbidding place.

Ivy had an idyllic childhood. He remembered his mother's soft dresses, all colored in pastels, as she would read fairy tales to him in French, German, and English. She was a beautiful woman who walked with graceful ease and a calm deportment, but with Ivy, she would run, chasing him through the village as he screamed in delight, showing no signs she cared about the disapproving glances she received. She hated turning her son over to the priests for school and, each day, would meet him at the gate to the church for some new adventure, as if the hours of separation had weighed on her. Perhaps they would walk down to the Seille river, and she would feed him a lunch of bread and cheese, then help him fish in the river for little silver flat fish. Or maybe they would help the baker bake bread or the potter make pots. When a wild and fey mood hit her, she would unearth her father's old cavalry carbine, and they would shoot dishes down at the archery butts with ammunition sold to her by reservists returning from annual maneuvers. Ivy never heard his mother speak of his father; his name was just a line on a paper he saw once, but she kept his picture on the piano and would at times pour herself a small glass of white wine and drink it, the picture standing next to her elbow. As for her father (his grandfather), the people in the village said he was mad. He had been swallowed up at Verdun with only the artillery carbine coming home to show he ever existed, leaving Ivy's mother under the care of the huge extended family.

Something about the loss of his father on Nanga Parbat made his mother detest the cold, and when he turned six, she fell in with a colonial agent and dragged him to Indochina. After that, each year, she would meet and be wooed by some other figure, but it was always one who was heading out to the extreme reaches of the world. Then for the six months of winter they would live in an exotic locale that their class and rank would not have normally allowed them to visit. She was always the young figure skater who had retained her beauty and youth. He was the son she loved who could always be at her side but who she indulged to allow out adventuring in the new lands they visited.

In 1938, he was 10 and ready for a new winter adventure when his mother announced that he must attend the academy in the South. Ivy was angry, but then he realized that she was doing it for his own good. He forgave her and went to school.

The war separated Ivy from his mother. She had been in Vic-Sur-Seille when the Germans annexed it, and Ivy was a 12-year-old student in the Academie d' St. Etienne. They exchanged letters, but the barriers imposed by the Germans were impossible to cross. What worried Ivy the most was that many ranking Germans were after his mother to serve as their wartime mistress. She did not want to be shackled to some NAZI, so her life became one of seclusion, avoiding the Germans as much as she could. Angry and impotent, Ivy joined the resistance.

More than one child from the Academie d' St. Etienne and the École de Tardy stepped away from classes to fight with the resistance, even though fighting often only meant counting troop trains as they passed through the city on the way to Italy. The Vichy were arbitrarily brutal, and many children, resistance or not, would disappear into the clutches of the Milice, never to be seen again.

Ivy's first job was to carry messages, organized by the old priest from Cathédrale Saint-Charles-de-Borromé, a man who taught Ivy many life lessons. It was well known the man was a pedophile, but it was also known that he had forsaken such acts to be a priest, and he never once treated any of the children he directed in the war uncivilly. Although for years he was hated by the people of Saint-Étienne, his bravery forced people to reconsider him. When he died, Ivy was promoted to active resistance where he would cross from fighting groups in the countryside to scouting in the city dressed as a schoolchild, an 11mm black powder revolver hidden in his pants. He was involved in several famous raids: derailing trains, marking targets for bombers, and one time, stealing rifles from the great St. Etienne armory, which allowed him to cast aside his ancient revolver for a semiautomatic rifle. He associated this feat with his own passage into manhood. He was 15 by the time the allies invaded.

After the tragic bombing of École de Tardy, Ivy was deemed too shell-shocked to be of use to the fighters around St. Etienne, so he was passed instead to a Jedburgh team who could use his English. He soon found himself being passed around resistance units, and finally, in October of 1944, he was transferred to the 26th Infantry Division of the United States Army as a guide and translator.

It was November of 1944 when the American division he worked with began a costly campaign to take Nancy, on the doorstep of his own place of birth. A division jeep dropped him off near the supply company of the 104th Infantry Regiment, and he went forward until he found a tank unit getting ready to assault the town of his birth.

Ivy often wondered what those tank drivers thought of him. He was a tall, thin, 16-year-old boy, pretending to be a man with a bottle of gin in his battle dress pocket, a cigar clenched in his teeth, and two civilian-style leather ammunition bandoliers crammed with rounds for his rugged five-shot autoloader. A tank driver, a huge black man with an American Tommy gun and a gold tooth, said to him, "Kid, this won't be pretty."

Ivy shrugged like he was a man of the world. Biting down on his cigar, he said, *"C'est prévu."*

Ivy, in his short life, had lived among the bravest men and women, people whom he knew faced the threat of horrible torture, life-altering mutilation, and deaths so final that their colleagues would never find what happened to them. Despite this, he soon found that the black soldiers fighting around his birthplace were the fiercest men he had ever met. They drove their tanks into a fierce line of resistance, destroying enemy positions and getting destroyed themselves. Ivy watched in wonder as the men abandoned one burning tank only to run back and climb into another, less injured vehicle, and when no tanks were left, they would fire machine guns and finally small American carbines at the enemy. It was like some mighty god had infused these men with the courage of seraphim.

After the tank unit forced the Germans out, Ivy went to find his mother. It was a trip of memory; he found people he had lived with as a child, cousins and former friends, hiding in basements, evacuated to a small glade of woods, and cowering in backyard bomb shelters. He found two German civilian GESTAPO men hiding with scared relatives and felt the surge of power as he unscrewed the tiny bayonet that equipped his rifle and prodded the German policeman into the street for the Americans to take into custody. Before, the people of his hometown had never really seen him as anything but an orphan child to a Czech commoner, having Protestant blood with the possible taint of German. Now, he was walking tall, rifle in hand, dirty from days of fighting, cigar clenched to his mouth, and a pair of American rifle grenades hanging from leather bandoliers of ammunition. They looked at him in amazement as he barked English back and forth with the immense black-skinned tankers and saluted the battalion commander from the 104th. He was a hero, returned to his home.

He had found his mother in a ditch by the river where she had taken refuge. How tiny she was, lying there as if asleep, wearing a pastel dress and a thick brown wool coat. The bullet that took her pierced her neck and was stippled with burn marks. Ivy stood up and said, "Someone did this to her." Then, he felt huge arms embracing him as he tried to break free to find the guilty party.

"You gotta swallow it some. You gotta put it away, use it when you need it. She would have wanted you to survive."

Ivy lifted his head up, embarrassed at crying, and saw that he was surrounded by a dozen grave, black faces. A leading sergeant stepped up. "You don't fall out, kid."

"I am not a kid."

REFUGEES OF VIRDEA

DATE: JANUARY 29, 2018
LOCATION: CONROY, MASSACHUSETTS

The club was dark, lit mostly by syncopating flashes of light timed to the music and by the chem lights patrons wore. Dutch club music, nameless and repetitive, blasted out from strategically mounted speakers, striking the strangely anechoic walls and occasionally fading in the bends of the twisting corridors that fed the three dance floors. I was adding to the glints of light by wearing a single red chem light and six that were dark. In fact, they were IR chem lights, which made this a pricey interview.

I was dressed dark in surgical scrubs onto which I had painted the O/Z symbol of Virdea with several t-shirts below that and dress slacks with red suspenders slung below the scrubs. The meeting was strange enough that I was carrying my ASP baton in an elastic band around my belt and a high-powered flashlight. It would be abandoned into my glove box when things turned out to be a little saner.

Sanity was a question. The whole club was a bizarre melange of styles and people. There was no music standard; one syncopating beat replaced the next, each time hinting at some popular music. It was like the DJ had lucked into a million royalty-free music drops and wanted to use them all. My own eyesight was giving me problems, and I could feel rather than see an orange aura at the sides of my sensorium.

The music changed to some Stephen Pilgrim, bass-heavy, leaping tune and the crowds started to jump as if each were hooked into a parallel switch that controlled their motion. I noticed one woman across the room that was not jumping. She was thin, with intense eyes and soft blond-white hair. When the crowd went down, she appeared, staring intensely. When it went up into the air, she disappeared.

I started a circuitous route to her and immediately lost her in the flailing of the crowd. My path took me by a deafening speaker when I felt a tap on my shoulder. I turned with a start, and she was standing behind me. I said hello, but she tapped her ears. I felt something behind me and turned. It was a larger man, not more than 35, with a sad face and a scholarly way of dressing. He lifted his jacket a little and revealed a taser. I turned back, and the blonde woman put a finger to her lips.

A tall, younger, black-bearded man appeared by my side while an older woman and man entered the circle. The tall man looked at me and asked the blonde woman, "Is he Virdea touched?"

"More than that, he is Virdea drawn. I wish the Seer was here."

Virdea drawn? Damn, I was having a seizure. I turned around, and space lagged behind, my vision stopping on the faces around me. One of the older men said, "Regulus, we have to get him back to the colony."

"We can. Is he dangerous?"

"Something has hold of him."

The one called Regulus said, "Carolina, Brian, take his arms like he is drunk."

Then, I was falling. I could not fly, though.

I was in a cage. There were water and rat entrails there for me and some straw that made a soft seat. The room I was in was a round tower. Windows open to the sky allowed plenty of daylight in, and I could see blue sky and clouds that I longed to fly among. The room was a madman's laboratory. An articulated human skeleton stood in a corner, the jawbone missing and replaced with a wire model. Books and scrolls were tossed across the space as if in response to a tornado. Wooden shelves lined the walls and crammed in every space was glassware filled with liquids, bric-a-brac, colored dust, living and dead insects, and swirling vapors. In the middle of the room, a man in a robe festooned with symbols was working on a spell.

"I know you are ridden, Master Raven. Speak. Your tongue will be translated."

"Woff?" I said.

He turned to me. "What does woff mean? It does not translate."

I replied, "You asked me to speak."

"Incorrect. You are a Fox-Bard, no?"

"Not even sure what a Fox-Bard is."

"You find out facts, then create a lie called news to keep an audience from discovering those facts. Like the clan of Fox-Bards."

"Then no, I am not one of those."

"What arc you, then?"

I thought. A raven's brain is roomy for an animal, but it is small for a human. Thinking was an effort, and words took time to form. "I am a writer specializing in magical hyper-narrative biomythical realistic meta-fiction."

"Who named you as this?"

"I named myself." I caught myself pulling a nit from my feathers and stopped myself. I was a bird, but humans do not chase lice in front of wizards.

"What does it mean?"

"Damned if I know. It sounds good in literary journals."

The Wizard grunted and then lit a taper from his work desk. The taper flared up, and he pushed it into the cage at me. I had to hop and jump about the cage to avoid it. He pulled it out and said, "Please talk sense."

"I am a writer, and I am writing a story about Virdea."

The Wizard turned and set up a little stone font. He seemed busy, almost too busy for me. He said to me as he worked, "From Earth?"

"Yes." Simple answers were so easy to say. I stretched a wing and hit the edge of the cage. *Fucking Wizard* was an easy thought to think. I ruffled my feathers a little and then used one eye to stare at my captor.

"Your magic is innate then, not learned?"

The Wizard was distracted by his nameless tasks. I watched as the Wizard was taking small charms from a wooden box and lining them up on one of his long wooden tables. He looked at them and then scowled. "I did not learn or even desire to have epilepsy. In fact, I take drugs to suppress it. The magic is killing me."

The Wizard turned and wrote down a series of figures in a codex-bound book. "Things are about to change for you now."

"Let me guess, roasted raven is a Virdean delicacy, and it's about time for Thanksgiving."

"Oh, no," the Wizard chuckled. "You are just about to be bound to me as my familiar. Your human body will die, but you will be immortal in Virdea. How many people in your sad land, I wonder, would commit any crime for the boon I am about to hand you."

"Do you need an answer?" I stopped and watched him work, slowly moving about his room like each task mattered. *What a lunatic,* I thought. *When I write your character, I will give you a foul body odor and jock itch.*

"Rhetorical, none needed." He stopped and sniffed the air, then scratched himself under his robes.

Forgetting my human self, I gave a raven skip of assent, dipping my nose and tilting my head. "And why give me this boon?"

"Your expertise in tracking a particular set of fugitives is reason enough. There are others. Right now, I desire my lost love above all else."

I skipped again in my cage, then remembered to use my words. "I do not think Rains-a-Lot is your type."

The Wizard glanced at me over his shoulder. "You want to be the jester, no doubt. You will not bait me. Dr. Kelle Brainerd is in love with me, and I will have her back at my side."

"Couples counseling is less expensive than enslaving unwilling authors and killing off their human forms. Besides, that is illegal."

The Wizard laughed again. "Not in New Hampshire."

"My body is in Massachusetts."

"Hard to tell from here."

Is that a joke? I watched as the Wizard wrote. Occasionally, he would go to his jars and carefully measure out some substance and put it into a parchment envelope. "Kelle is a wizard, you know."

"I did not."

"She uses math and science. Called herself a Stem Wizard. She found in training that she could be quite powerful." The Wizard went to a book, flipped through its pages, and then began to practice some hand gestures. "She made me more powerful. You see, magic is the gating of power from another plane to help you perform some work. That is all. A wizard learns a great mass of information before they can cast their first spell."

"The problem is that a lot of what we learn is only helpful in getting the human mind into a place where it can handle the surge of power that it must channel. And not all of that learning is actually valid. It is tradition and works like a sugar pill on the ignorant. Some of that technique is useful as hell, but not for gating magic, just for keeping your mind in the right place. And some techniques can be useful far beyond their expense."

I was listening, the Wizard was lonely and chattering to a bird, which was kind of pathetic, but my mind was divided. A great snowy owl hand landed on a sill, quiet as a ghost. She turned to me and, in bird-sign, said, "Quiet."

The Wizard began to drone again, and I watched as the great owl slowly made its way to my cage. It had a clever beak, opening up the cage gate and letting me pass through. She and I then took wing. The scream of an angry wizard came from the tower behind us.

"Keep out of his hands until we can be called from Virdea!" the owl screeched. I followed her lead. I opened my wings wide and sculled with strength and power the air. The wind was passing by me with a muted roar, but my ears corrected for the great rush of sound.

The wizard's tower was a construct of magic, a black needle 100 meters tall and 30 meters across. It stood in the center of 144 hexagons, and those hexagons were surrounded in turn by a crenelated shield wall. The hexagons were each filled with one thing: a garden, a house, or an open area, creating a beautiful mix of man-made and natural colors and shapes. I became lost in the pattern until my rescuer yelled, "Monkey bats!"

I ducked my head into the air stream and said, "Fuck." It came out as an unearthly screech. Issuing forth from one of the hexes was a small cloud of flying creatures. My eyes, sharp as ever, made out their gibbous faces, fanged teeth, clawed arms, and legs, and their wings beating a tattoo on the wind. "You've got to be shitting me."

"What?" My rescuer screamed. We were each struggling to gain altitude, breast muscles beating the thick air, searching for an updraft. The bats were a hundred meters behind. "Those are Siamangs!"

With wings, I appended in my mind. A meter long and 12 kilograms, like an African bustard. Who the fuck thought those things were good ideas? I turned in the air and dove.

I did not have the wings of a gyrfalcon, nor the breast muscles of an albatross. My wings were not thin wedges like that of a swift nor were they designed for their aspect ratio, like a teal. I was a raven. Not just any raven, but a Great Raven of Virdea. I am 3 kilograms of muscle, heavy enough that only the great eagles bother us as all in the air. I can dive at 90 km/h with my claws outstretched and attack four times before I must turn skyward again. I am not the greatest bird, the fastest bird, the most graceful bird, the highest-flying bird, the heaviest bird, or the prettiest bird, but I am the bird that is all things. Only the parrot is my equal in my eyes.

My mind was not all human. I could feel the struggle of the human brain to fit into the space of the Raven brain, the tiny allotted area for intellect. My brain contained so many things, many of them remembered like a dancer remembers dance steps. As I gained speed, I could feel my feathers tense up to regulate the rate I accelerated while my tail muscle bunched and began to bite the air, giving me maneuverability.

I recognized in my dive that the flying Siamangs were not monkeys, but bats—magically bloated and hardly as dangerous as they looked. Some human had said, "What can I create that will cause as much terror as possible?" Then, they had morphed some poor woodland creature into this.

My pressure sense could feel the owl had followed me in the dive. She was the most silent of birds and the most accurate of divers. Together, we dove on the creatures, trading slip-streams and guiding each other in. I could sense her slight sculls in the slipstream and edged up my leading feathers to quiet the airflow.

Down we dove, faster and faster, then we collided with the benighted creatures. The trick with them was easy. They had claws, but no power in either their dives or recovery. Their wings were clever, so you could not spill their air and cause them to crash, but you could cost them altitude that they would never make back, and they had no way to touch you.

I pulled out of my crashing dive just above the monkey-bats, claws stretched, and flipped one then another into the airstream with a shuddering crash. They tried to catch air, but this was a mistake as the owl caught them from behind with her killing claws and tore their vulnerable mammal necks out.

A big Siamang thought he had my measure as he flipped in the air, but I had his, the vulnerable gray-streaked pink skin yielded to my claws. I felt the thrill of my raking slash, how my sharp claws retracted as they bit skin to keep me from tangling in the flesh of my prey while doing maximum damage to the evil creature I was raking. It screeched in an ululation of pain and fear. As the monkey-bat fell, I ported and sideslipped around him and then traded some altitude for speed.

"Head for the sea!" the owl yelled on the wind. It was hard to think logical thoughts, but her meaning was clear. I let my head swivel in the slipstream of my increasing airspeed and saw that my victories were short-lived. For each bat I chased from the air, two were rising from the wizard's tower. Logic was a hard thought pattern to practice when you were only half in your right mind, but even a raven can see the inescapable truth of the advantage a predator has over prey. I put my beak back into the wind flow and beat my powerful wings as fast as I could to gain even more velocity; the owl kept up wing scull for wing scull, slightly behind me to take advantage of the turbulence I generated moving through the air.

Once out over the ocean, the white owl said, "Be ready, I can feel them pulling us back."

"Who?"

"The commune. The Seer."

With a flash, I crashed onto a couch in an industrial sleeping loft. The loft was tall, perhaps 10 meters, with huge windows shaded in the darkness of night. It was packed with old-style printing presses, figures standing in darkened corners, and a huge collection of books, numberless and stacked in rickety piles. A woman crashed down onto a couch across from me, the white owl turned out to be a blonde woman whom I had met in the bar named Sarah Cravies.

The people in the room began to care for Sarah and me, cautiously, as if each of us could sprout a tail any minute and proceed to eat every human we found. A tall, thin woman with gray hair and sharp features was standing by, holding what looked like a bastard sword casually in her hand. A man with, of all things, a Hogwarts-type wand walked up and offered me tea, then introduced himself as Warhammer.

In the gloomy dark, an older woman sat with a black cane in a knitted shawl and a pullover sweatshirt. She peered at me with wise eyes as I vibrated, still not over being a bird. My breast muscles hurt, and my heart raced as I rapidly looked around the loft, hoping to see a route to the open sky. My eyes still darted around the room like I was hunted. "Virdea touched, what is your name?" she asked.

"McKeeby." I replied.

"You are vulnerable. You have the attention of one of the great powers of Virdea. A named power. The Wizard of the Obsidian Tower!" The old woman almost growled this, tapping her cane for emphasis, and the shadowy people in the room drew back. I could only blink at her.

Regulus, the tall German, caught my attention. "Think of Virdea like a cowboy story. Wild Bill, Custer, Sitting Bull. They all are names that have meaning. Virdea is a place where reputation and fame are directly related to magic."

"And what about you people?" I asked with a winded effort.

The German shrugged, "Virdea sucks in people from around the world, from many times. People of Earth are constantly, in small numbers, visiting Virdea. After days, years, or centuries, most humans come back to Earth. They are so changed there is little left for them anywhere else, so many take up art, trying to find a way to understand what they have experienced. Maybe they want to try and make the world better based on what they know." Regulus made a motion, including the whole room. "Everyone here has been Virdea touched, there is no going back on that. And that drives what we do. Many become artists."

"Or shuffleboard players," the one known as Bevan said to a round of laughter.

"Was that a Virdean bar?" I asked.

Bevan considered. "That? No, it's just a bar. If you find one of the gathering places for the Virdea touched, you will know it."

"I am writing a book."

Regulus said, "The Cat Keeper told us. You are telling a quest story. There are many of those, few ever get told."

The Seer leaned into the light, and the room went silent. "The best thing we can do for your story is to protect you from the Wizard and offer you what information we can on how to survive in Virdea." She reached behind herself and pulled out my walking stick, Grandfather. "This arrived shortly before you."

I took the stick from her. "Grandfather is never really lost, is he?"

"No, not this Grandfather. And once I see to the Wizard, Grandfather will protect you from him also."

THE SEER AND THE WIZARD

DATE: JANUARY 30, 2018
LOCATION: CONROY, MASSACHUSETTS

The Wizard of the Obsidian Tower found his sleep fitful. He was angry that he had failed to capture Kelle on Earth even after tracking her to 1960, Kansas. He had detected that she was the focus of scrying of the most powerful and subtle type, and when he captured the voyeur, he escaped with magical help. Meanwhile, Kelle was kicking up a storm across Virdea. By killing the Yellow King, she and her companions had triggered cataclysmic conflicts that were churning all of the lands. Some people were blaming him.

And he could detect the subtle power of one of the Nine. The Nine were the greatest named wizards of the lands of Virdea, the people whose magical power truly topped the others. The Wizard of the Obsidian Tower, his given name was Judius, was a member of the Nine due to his lifetime mastery of the craft of magic, and because he was willing to use this magic to the advancement of his own personal power.

The Wizard was not alone. He sat up and stared into the distance. It was the Seer.

"Judius." Her voice was mellow, wise, elfin, and soft. She was present in his bedroom not in physical form, but as an ethereal construct. The Wizard did not feel fear, the Nine rarely if ever battled each other directly and thus he was in little real danger, but he was perturbed by the effrontery the Seer showed. She stood in his inner sanctum, a dark figure bathed in light, her gods be-damned cane tapping the floor nervously like with the sound of a tap dancer who had lost the taps from one or her shoes. "Seer." He said, reaching subtly with his left hand for a wand.

"You have been busy this year," she said. She was dressed in a white and gray jogging suit, human modern, and had her damnable black cane, which she insisted on tapping impatiently.

"I was wondering which master of magic would grace me. So does the Circus Covenatus, the Contract of Gold stand?"

She laughed and waved her walking stick at him. "Did I come here to do battle? Oh Judius, even as a snot nose you were dramatic. The wizards do not compete to destruction." Judius relaxed a little. The idea of the Covenatus has been simple in the past. Nine of the most powerful practitioners of magical arts agreed to turn their destructive internecine fighting into something of a game, moving pawns on a chess board.

"Then why are you here?" He knew why; he wanted her to say it.

"Oh, Judius." She slapped her cane on the ground. "How many times must I tell you Earth is not your playground?" She walked around his bedroom, staring at his magical wards and canteries that were, theoretically at least, protecting him from her use of magic despite the contract. She seemed unimpressed, which annoyed Judius to no end, especially when she lifted the visor on a suit of armor onto which he had imbued a guards and wards spell.

The Nine were competitors but they were supposed to be brethren. In the complexities of personal relationships in a land ruled by reputation, the Nine were simply people who agreed to avoid competition that would prove destructive, not all competition. When wizards play chess, it is said, the chessboard melts. Instead, they direct the hands that play chess.

Enough, he thought. He stood up from his bed and went to his tea service. A minor charm started a fire on the water heater, and he also covered his first casting of a spell that was perfectly within bounds to cast, but which the Seer would not like at all. "I have lost a valuable possession. That possession was to be found on Earth. I pursued that possession and have found that one of those Earthlings you claim to protect is in fact a creature of the interface."

"You lost a woman," she replied as if Kelle was just a woman, or as if she was replaceable by any measurement of that mundane term.

"More than that." He growled. The old witch was tapping her cane and walking in a rough circle around his hexagon-shaped bedroom, as distracted and awful as she always was. Why couldn't she attend to her looks like the Queen of Fire and Ice? That bipolar bitch at least looked like a million Tolars. The Seer looked like she should be peeling potatoes in some peasant hovel.

She looked at him with her eagle eyes. "Worth bringing a magical catastrophe to Earth?"

He turned back. The spell he was forming was made in making tea. Each movement of the tea ceremony advanced the power in a subtle way, undetectable except by someone who knew the ceremony precisely. "I did no such thing."

There was disapproval from the Seer's voice and she tapped her cane in a staccato of taps, like a pissed-off dancing master. "Lying? What of Bashful?"

"Bashful no longer exists. I erased it from the minds of men." That had been a feat. Humans were so smug with their science and their Xbox Windows Joystick things and their protective Donkey Kongs, that they had no idea so much could be robbed of them, so quickly, and so silently. He had relished taking an entire town and turning it into rumor.

The Seer radiated pique, maybe even anger from where she stood near his library. "You are starting to hurt the playing board. If you wreck the board, where will the pieces play? If you move too fast, push too hard, we all know how cracks in time grow!"

The Wizard said, "You are growing old Earth-time, Seer. Do you have time to scold me?" As the water boiled, he cut the tea with a fine knife, 13 times and then 13 more. He could feel the growing power with the smell of the gunpowder tea. He thought of when he showed the magic of the tea ceremony to Kelle, how she had reveled in it, and he felt an erection coming on. Only the presence of the Seer stopped that reverie. The old fucking hag. "Do you have the power to stop me from doing what I want?"

Then he felt, icily, her power come down on him. "Of course," the Seer said, "you are the more powerful. However, I have my skills. My gesa says you will not bring harm down on the observer known as Nelson McKeeby. Some of us are looking to him to tell this story. And that should concern you."

He screamed, "Fuck!" The old bitch had been deactivating his wards with the taps of her cane, and he had been too busy to tell. His own tea ceremony spell, which would have restricted her to Earth for 111 days, collapsed, and he felt a small tightening of his world, a restriction of his options. It was a gesa.

A gesa was a spell that protected some person or object from harm by another being. It was powerful magic but with great limitations. In this case, tradition made it a powerful tool. The Seer had, in essence, claimed Nelson McKeeby as her henchman quaestor, and thus provided her protection, which was more powerful when directed against someone who had signed covenants.

Judius threw off his dressing gown and blazed forth in battle magic, facing the Seer in all of her power and glory. And a third being was present. Standing in the corner of his room was the enigmatic Darkness. He always appeared in an impeccably tailored English business suit with a bowler, but in place of hands and a face, oily smoke poured from his clothing. On the day the covenant was signed, it was before the dangerous Darkness, Master of the Great Spaces, Counter of Time, Lord of the Wastes, who witnessed and guaranteed the document. It was that or destroy the world in war.

Darkness spoke in his pedantic, almost cloying voice. "I have spent so much time bothered by who was directed the Sorcerer Cinnamon, that perhaps I have not paid enough attention to either of you in recent years."

The blinding light of the Seer and Judius's own blazing head toned down a little. Judius pointed at the Seer and said, "She stole a piece from the board."

The Seer replied, "An Earthling piece, my calling."

Judius responded, "A Virdea touched, in play by the covenant."

Darkness said, "Silence."

Judius was offended that this hack, this Old Being from the farthest memory of the universe, should interfere. "You have no right, Darkness, when the covenant is unbroken."

Darkness moved forward in the terrible, slow, floating movement he always affected. "Grow some fucking feet and use them." Judius tried to think, but he was interrupted by a constriction in his mind quite like someone closing off his throat of air, but this constriction forced his thoughts to back up and tumble about the floor of his intellect. "Shut," Darkness said, pausing, "up."

Judius had no option but to comply. When the Seer seemed about to say something, Darkness raised a smokey hand, and she also fell to silence.

"Who is this Mortal?" he asked. The constriction on Judius's mind eased a small amount.

"A human writer, Virdea touched. One of the Oz it seems."

Darkness paused for a second. His suit was perfect in all ways. A lover of human art would be forgiven for thinking that he should have an apple in place of his smoking face, but this was merely folly that was holding back Judius from screaming in fear. When you became a power in Virdea, a name, it was easy to forget some names were infinite in their power simply because they refrained from using it. If wizards melted chess boards, Darkness melted continents. Darkness slowly spoke. "He is a Swami? Has Rumi generated another of his great thinkers?"

The Seer answered, "He is touched, but he is dying. He translates but cannot make the leap himself. The mortal will destroy himself soon."

"Then what is he to each of you?"

Judius said, "He holds the key to one of my lost pieces."

"The only key."

Lying to Darkness was impossible. "No."

He turned to the Seer. "And why do you interfere with the game play of your brother?"

"The piece is innocent. Writer. He may be useful in telling humans about the lands of the greater space. He sees the stories of Virdea and writes them with a keen awareness."

"Is he an entertaining writer?"

"No," the Seer said. "He rushes the story, pushes into where he need not go. Confuses his message in side notes."

"Then why protect him?"

"He is better than nothing?" The Seer, for a second, radiated embarrassment.

Darkness laughed and released the Wizard. "Then, I will solve both of your problems. What is the name of this writer?"

"Nelson McKeeby, of Spirit Lake, Iowa," the Seer admitted.

"He is my piece now. You are both advised to leave him be." With that, he was gone.

Judius looked at the Seer in disgust. "See what you did?"

She replied, "Shut up."

THE UNIVERSAL PRIMER

DATE: SEPTEMBER 16, 2016
LOCATION: TAMPA, FLORIDA

(Excerpt from the lab notebooks of
Dr. Kelle Brainerd)

It is amazing the risks scientists take: risks that make my own explorations into time and space seem tame in comparison. Take, for example, Dr. Anatoli Brouchkov. Thinking himself completely immortal, and having nothing else to do (he must have completely run out of scientifically valid experiments to conduct), Dr. Brouchkov one day decided to try out some ancient bacteria. You see, he had access to some Bacillus F, which was supposedly found in permafrost that was 3.5 million years old. Now, I tend to think the stuff was actually scrapped off the bottom of some Russian cold fusion reactor, but my mind is rather dark regarding scientific hoaxes. In any case, this genius takes the barely understood bacteria and injects it into himself.

There are three possibilities here. The sample was fake and genius-boy was not in danger, never having opened his system to a stray life form. The second is that the sample was real and genius-boy dodged a pretty big bullet. The third is that the sample not only is real but also could be mutating in genius-boy's system, and when it finds a key to the current primate immune system, it will burst forth and ravage human society as we know it. If a zombie apocalypse occurs, good bet it was Anatoli who acted as patient zero.

Maybe nothing will happen, but science is a powerful tool and entails risks. One of those risks is that idiots looking for headlines can cause terrible things to happen if they do not watch it. In writing this rather tame and barely scientific missive I intend to open up the discussion of reality physics, but I want to do it in a perfectly understandable way. Reality physics is really scary, and many of the maps we follow have big blank spots where the mapmaker has said, "Here be dragons."

During the 1920s, radiation study took on a certain vogue. Famous and wealthy people traveled to the radioactive springs in Europe to have radioactive materials pumped into their bodies. Oddly enough, sometimes these treatments increased the health of the person receiving them. We know that some diseases can be shoved into body-extinction because they mutate rapidly when exposed to low levels of radiation. Since the range of possible genetic drift for micro-organisms includes far more paths to senescence than to increased morbidity, the gamble is that the micro-organism, whose gene editing routines are simple, will more likely run down a dead end when exposed to radiation than the other extreme. Thus, radiation poisoning at low levels depends on the human remaining more resilient than the germ or virus being treated. In some ways, injecting oneself with penicillin is the same bet, that the body's allergy system won't kill the larger organism before it kills the smaller.

That brings us to William J. A. Bailey. He was a fraud on the same level as Elizabeth Holmes, who invented specious medical treatments and sold them to a gullible public.

These treatments were not only often ineffective (in the larger sense that whatever benefits gained from being poisoned by huge doses of radioactive metals are quickly consumed by the downsides of such poisoning) but also deadly on a large scale. Worse, they opened society to that old hidden danger of subjecting the human body to odd situations like radiation poisoning, which also opened a possible gate through which apocalyptic disease may charge through.

The one thing that Bailey did for us in his idiotic maundering was to create a new mathematics of danger. Given unknown and unknowable outcome A, what is the chance that action B will result in reaction C (a beneficial outcome) or reaction Z (massive destruction of human life)? The math said that many people would have small harms and some would have small benefits, and there was a small chance that radiation poisoning would open a vector for a super germ to wipe humans off the face of our planet.

To see how this math works, think of the atom bomb. During the planning for the Trinity Tests in 1943, Enrico Fermi reviewed the math behind a nuclear chain reaction running out of control. During his work, he humorously took bets on the first test, with money being placed on three results, 1) the bomb would destroy the planet, 2) the bomb would destroy the state of New Mexico, 3) the math was correct, and it would explode as expected. This was just grim humor, as it was almost mathematically impossible for the atom bomb to result in a solar phoenix consumption of the planet (and here I stress almost… since it was possible). They lit off the bomb and the results were a predictable range of benefits and problems.

My own field of reality physics plays in deep waters. A tornado is one of the densest energy events that naturally occur, creating around 3 x 1019 ergs. Yet this energy density is enough to bend and even break the Cherkov space-time barrier. Take an even more energy-dense event, such as one that occurs in the chamber of a particle accelerator, where there could be a point that the Cherkov barrier is not bent but broken in a way that cannot be repaired, and all sorts of interesting things happen. One second, a scientist is proudly hitting the red button as others around him or her pop champagne. The next second, depending on the command and control delay, the scientist and everything within 100 miles of the lab is accelerating at relativistic speeds in a newly created event horizon. Not a good outcome if you have a mortgage and two-point-one kids who are rapidly falling behind you in a more or less fixed space-time continuum.

So my own research has always been a bit hesitant and perhaps even retarded. I built my first time-traveling chamber, a small accelerator nexus, when I was 16. It could move an object back in time nearly a minute. It proved impossible to keep up with, and I had to destroy it. I would be sitting in my lab and a copy of Tolstoy would show up in the nexus. That meant I had to both find my own duplicate copy of the book, then put it into the nexus, then re-shelve the original book.

The danger of this device was that it became my master, rather than me being its master. A cosmic joke, and I was its tiny butt. However, the power involved with reality science and what can be gained by using that power is immense, so I did not stop there; I simply did more math.

When I discovered Virdea, after five years of hard work, I duplicated something that had been done before. People, for years, have been disappearing into windstorms and ending up elsewhen. Heck, once an entire navy ship ducked into Virdea for a short bit. I just opened a portal through which I could step. That portal was difficult to keep open, imprecise, and fitful, but it proved a long series of math I had done, trying to make sure I did not destroy the universe. And much to my chagrin, it had been done before.

On October 30, 1968, Dustin-Rhodes Company scientists used what is known as a Reality Collider to attempt to create a gateway into another world. They had made similar attempts before with odd results, and the rumor has always said they had some pretty strange ways of opening these theoretical gates that they kept unpublished. This time, though, they made the attempt. And they shattered the Cherkov barrier. The scientists stood in fear as a rip started in the reality of space/time, tearing people apart, causing wild hallucinations, and bending space in bizarre ways. Finally, the three surviving scientists were huddled in the corner of the laboratory waiting for the slowly advancing time-space rip to consume them before going on to make a meal of the rest of the world when a being in a dark suit, his skin made from oily black vapor, strode through the rent and stopped its growth. The being then turned to the scientists and, in a British accent, said, "Do not do that again." He then disappeared.

Dustin Rhodes closed that facility and wiped it from memory, but I found hints and suggestions about it. I only wonder if my own research will one day result in a visit from the man with smoke for skin? Or have I taken the right path in my research on Virdea, moving to understand the world I can port to? My dad, for all of his intelligence, dismisses my work. He sees it as a colossal waste of money that since it keeps his precocious daughter occupied and off Tinder, he is happy to spend it.

Which brings us to why I think Virdea exists. The power of reality physics is so profound that I think the universe needs a pressure shunt to keep reality on its toes. Where have all the dragons gone? Send them to Virdea before humans invent fighter planes and things get messy. It is more profound though than that. I think one of the reasons that God created Virdea was to allow humanity a place to escape from the reality that they face by their own hands. Maybe I am wrong, though.

HOLLOW MEN

DATE: 3RD DAY OF THE RAM, 3684
LOCATION: CLAYTON FISK, VIRDEA

It was at mealtime that Ivy often felt the weight of distance from his past press down on him. It made him realize that he had no "normal" from which to compare the habits of others. In his earliest years traveling with his mother, he remembered hot semolina donuts shared with the children of his mother's driver, dipped in honey if they were lucky, and stolen sips of black coffee, tiny tastes that would still send him into space with hyperactivity.

A year later, it was mofo gasy, thick round pancakes served by the house staff of an admiral his mother had grown fond of. If they scrubbed the odd, dimpled pan it was made in, the cook would delight them with the puffy pancakes, pouring an extravagant amount of sweetened condensed milk on top of each one and letting them lick the plate as if they were street urchins.

And a year past that, it was the inspector of ports that his mother had wooed, and that gentleman's household was fed from a restaurant. The children of the compound, Ivy, and the scion of house servants, would eat breakfast with the service staff consisting of Xoi with fried peanuts. They were often given a sweet banana if they were well-behaved and a ball of rice for the lunch meal.

This is where Ivy became distressed about his own personal lack of a culture he could consider "his." Everywhere he went, the people of the land had their own ways of living, but Ivy could call none of them his. French for him was just a language, to be replaced when needed by Vietnamese, Italian, Algerian, Malagasy, English, or even German. He dreamed in all of these languages, which worried him. He thought at least your dreams should be unique to your own tribe.

Virdea was again awakening the feelings of him being a stranger in a familiar universe. The people of the land ate pies of meat and vegetables, toothsome stews of barley or peas cooked with salt pork, pottages of grain onto which milk or beer had been poured, or sops where bread was dipped in wine, cheese, or drippings. At each stop, they bartered for food and were fed from the larder of a people who lived by the land and worked hard for every mouthful. These people were primarily farmers and artisans before anything else, and their meals reflected the simplicity of the people and the rigors of their lives.

It could describe his own family if one ignored his immediate parents. His mother had a precision mind that thought in lines cut in ice, not in dirty soil. His father, it was said, thought only of the next mountain to master until he froze to death trying to master the last one. Still, when she returned home in 1938 it was to help with the family estate and prepare for the war everyone assumed was coming. Despite this, it was years later, in Indochina, before the idea of being a farmer struck Ivy. In the turmoil of hate that was the Indochinese conflict, the farmers got up each morning and tended their crops. Battles delayed but did not stop harvests. The war to feed the world was a war that was as endless as the one Ivy fought in the paddies and mountainsides, only victory in that war was nourished life for others, rather than bloody death. Ivy could no longer eat a breakfast without thinking about where it came from. And that again turned him inward as he came from nowhere.

A wan villager, all angles, dressed in a brown hooded cassock, stopped before his table. "More mush?" she asked.

'No, thank you."

The village was run by a group that called themselves the Hetman. They were, to say the least, a vulgar lot. "Maricia is sweet on the outlander, no?" He laughed cruelly. "Fuck if she offers me another helping of this horrible glop." This particular Hetman was named Glabius, and he was what Kelle called a dick.

Across the table, Rains-a-Lot put his fork down, an ominous sign. Ivy said, "Clayton Fisk certainly grows a lot of pumpkins."

Glabius said, "A fuck load, and damn good you came by or they would wither on the vine. We cannot sell them to the city-states because the troubles have stopped travel on the main rivers and the turnpikes. No one will pay for pumpkins that are not in the feed lot."

Ivy looked down at his plate. It was a hash of barley and pumpkin dressed with a fish sauce from the delta. The locals grew a range of gourds, three types of savory pumpkins, and a sweet pumpkin whose sugar content rivaled beets. It was the last that they had bought by the hundreds of bushels in exchange for Kelle's hoarded silver coins. She was now busily producing alcohol to run the Chevy on. Ivy was still not sure how the engine of a 1957 Chevy could be tricked into running smoothly on alcohol, but Kelle had handled that as well as creating a still that seemed to be preternaturally efficient at converting mashed pumpkin pulp into ethanol.

"Did you hear my question?" Glabius asked.

Ivy shook his head. "No, I did not."

"You are making brandy?" he questioned with a sneer. As if making pumpkin brandy was a secret that would be important to anyone.

"Sort of," Ivy said. "Better distilled. Several hundred liters we hope."

"Why not share some with the Fisk?" The man was very pushy and ignorant.

Rains-a-Lot had pulled a flat stone and started stropping one of the T-56 bayonets. Ivy said, "That may be possible. I would have to ask Dr. Brainerd."

He laughed at Ivy. "She pretty much has your nuts in her coin pouch, no?"

"Sure." Ivy was feeling the pressure to get up and leave, but Kelle had warned them to treat the village leaders with respect.

"Gotta learn you up, pigeon." He made a sudden reach and had Maricia in his hands. She tried to struggle for a second, then remembered something, and went limp.

"Looks like we have our own little 'me too' moment." It was Kelle walking up with several of the farmers. Like Ivy and Rains-a-Lot, she was covered in vine stubble and dirt from the backbreaking labor, made harder by the knowledge of the forces gathering against them. She fixed Ivy with a stare and shook her head. Ivy let his muscles relax and removed his hand from his Browning.

"Brainerd, your pumpkins are to your satisfaction?" Glabius held onto the young woman like she was a party favor or a disposable cup.

"Mister Glabius, you are welcome to rule your village as you see fit, but your bawdry is inconvenient." Kelle was angry as hell and clipping her words precisely.

"How so?" The man's voice was oily, his lack of education flowing out even through the barrier of translation.

Kelle slapped her hand on the table and the room went quiet. "You are fucking up my magic, that is 'how so.' Magic requires a careful balance of the universe, call this balance the force. Your men are behaving in ways that disturb the force. I saw one beating a farmer, and I am sure sexual assaults are occurring. They must stop. How can the force be with us when you behave like gibbons?"

To the mundane, Ivy thought, *arguments of magic are trump cards*. Pumpkin wine takes three weeks minimum to make, but Kelle was making burnable pumpkin liquor in less than 40 hours. It had to be magic, but there was no way to know what might harm or help the spells. All of her talk of this "force" that ruled the universe and required balance was new to him. It was like she was making it up as she went along or reading it from some bad school play.

"The fuck you say?" the Hetman said.

"The fuck I say," Kelle replied.

"Perhaps you fuck off and leave our pumpkins alone."

"And take the silver."

There were a few seconds of silence. Glabius finally said, "Bitch," threw the woman he was clutching to the floor, and stalked off.

Kelle looked at Ivy and Rains-a-Lot. "Are you on union hours?"

Ivy glanced at Rains-a-Lot who was pushing the buds of Kelle's spare iPod into his ears. The Lakota had his top hat, which he perched on his head.

Carts dragged by villagers crisscrossed the fields, disturbing grounded flights of ravens and picking up pumpkins. When they were filled to the top, they were carried to ground tarps onto which they were dumped, where mallet-wielding farmers glumly smashed them and loaded the mash into barrels. Kelle would come by each barrel and add a starter to the batch, then she directed someone to drag the barrel close to a fire with a mass of others. The mash would then be reseeded with a new seed stock and heated again. After a few cycles, it would be dumped into a giant copper kettle purchased several weeks ago and dragged about on a cart for this purpose. Properly tended, the setup was producing several liters of 80% alcohol per hour.

The ruling hetman farmed from horseback but said little to their farmers. They just seemed to be some sort of guards rather than actual farmers and were prone to violent outbursts that Ivy tried to help Kelle control. To increase the efficiency, Ivy and Rains-a-Lot finally took over crews of farmers in the farthest fields, but even then the farmers of the Fisk were not very enthused, which was odd considering the economic situation they faced and the fact they were getting almost 100 grams of silver per finished liter of alcohol, about twice the normal street value of the crop delivered to a city-state 50 kilometers away would fetch.

He had taught the farmers to yell "need help" in English when they needed extra hands to tackle some aspect of the harvest, so when he heard several of the farmers yelling that he went to check it out. One of the farmers was on the ground so Ivy dropped his chopper and ran immediately to help. Somehow he must have tripped because he did not remember anything after that.

It was dark when he woke, stripped naked and arms and legs bound. There was a tailing fire burning, and hundreds of farmers stood around him of all ages and genders. A man in a stiff jute cloak and hempen skirtle, holding a staff on which an image of an old man had been carved, said, "It is our tradition to give any condemned the right of speech."

Ivy did not struggle. If he went missing too long, there was a freight train in the form of Rains-a-Lot in this direction, a calamity that these poor farmers could not possibly comprehend. If they killed him, that freight train would jump the tracks like a nuclear bomb and reign terror onto them. Rains-a-Lot, like Ivy, had been noting how odd this village was, and wondering what was going on here that they did not understand, but that wondering would end if one of them was harmed.

The clearing was filled with villagers, which meant they were not in town, and Ivy doubted they were stealthy enough to sneak into the woods as a group and not leave a trail. Ivy had to stall for time. "Is it the tradition to provide evidence to support condemnation?" Ivy asked.

"You are aiding our captors."

"The Hetmen, your village leaders?"

"Before six weeks ago, they were almost unknown to us. The revolutions spreading across the plains have pushed many from their normal sleeping spots. And many a bad person flees worse, only to land upon the innocent. I am Maynard of Fisk Clayton, and together with sister Danion and brother Origien, we are the true rulers of the Fisk."

Ivy wriggled in his bonds then was able to push himself into a more comfortable position. "If Dr. Brainerd knew of your predicament, Maynard, I doubt she would hesitate to act."

"She was informed. The task she has set us, that is her only concern." The man spoke in a stilted manner, as if the lowland tongue was foreign to him, or he was not very well educated.

Ivy looked at the man with a piercing gaze. "Bullshit."

"An expression of doubt I do not care for." The man had a curved knife in his hands. "Sentence to be carried out," he said.

Ivy struggled to his knees, "You want to see how a Frenchman dies? So be it." Ivy was heartbroken that he could not remember the words to La Marseillaise. He truly was from nowhere. It had to be one of Kelle and Rains-a-Lot's rock ballads. He closed his eyes and began to sing in a screaming voice "Gimme Shelter" by The Rolling Stones.

Behind Ivy's eyelids, he sensed a mocking presence fill his heart with coldness and an agitation among the ravens. The clearing was no longer alive with the sounds of hundreds of humans, but now was hyper-focused on the breathing of a single man and the metallic clank of a second. He opened his eyes and saw the orange-skinned Wizard that had chased them into Virdea. By his side was an armored man with the symbol of a burning wolf on his shield, standing at the head of a column of soldiers. The warrior's armor was lacquered in fine yellow and black, making him look like a mechanical bee walking on its hind legs, the effect though was ruined by an attempt to make his winged helmet look like a screaming wolf.

The Wizard was dressed very differently now than when they had encountered him in Bashful, Kansas. He wore blue cowboy boots, leather pants, a red pearl-buttoned shirt, and a leather vest. On his head was a tan, felt Stetson, high-crowned, with a blocked, wide brim. A yellow bandanna clashed with the Wizard's orange skin.

"He does not look to be much," the armored knight said. The farmers were ducking away in fear as the man walked forward, dragging a great sword behind him with obvious disdain.

The Wizard stopped and replied, "He is a valued henchman, nothing more. He has no reputation."

Ivy cursed in French, then switched to English, "I will happily sort you lot."

The Wizard laughed. "I am sorry, my knight. Lupufocu here understands you are a worm on a hook. I need to call out for your mistress. Tell her it is her beloved Judius Ronceville, Wizard of the Black Tower, who requires her presence."

"Even if I could, I would do no such thing." Ivy stuck his chest out and screamed hatred and defiance in a wordless yell out into the dark forest.

The cowboy-wizard waved off such trivia with his left hand. Lupufocu made a langorish motion and pushed his sword into the coals of the fire.

"You will ruin your temper," Ivy said.

The forest sounds had subsided. Gone were the ravens and the pestrals, cavies, and tiny berms. Instead, there was the hollow sound of the world reminding the listener that there was no such thing as quiet. The sword came out of the fire glowing cherry red. Lupufocu looked madly into the glow of the steel and said, "I ruined my temper long ago."

Ivy looked at the smoldering blade. "Torturing me won't make her come to you."

Lupufocu said, "The Wizard looks for fool's gold. I win a crown today." He then applied the blade to Ivy's shin.

Henri Alleg, a journalist arrested during the Algerian War, published in 1958 a book called La Question, about his captivity and torture by French paratroopers. Ivy was unique in some ways of having known both the people who tortured Alleg, and Alleg himself before the events ever happened. The paratroopers he knew had scars on their souls caused by 20 years of war fighting for their nation. Some of the men who wielded the torturer's blade had been tortured themselves by Vietnamese, Koreans, Japanese, Thai, or Germans. They all had fought enemies that had themselves lost their honor long ago. After a while, a man whose home fades into a memory, a being who lives with pain and death for too long and who does not have some form of humanity reinforced on his soul, becomes a hollow man bereft of some part of his own sanity and empathy. The hollow men who tortured Alleg did not even ask what the torture provided them, they just knew that if they hung on the same hook, they could expect torture as well. It was what all torturers told themselves, that they were doing this for a reason that made sense. It was what they told themselves at night when the demons of memory tore at their soul.

Torture, aside from some basic forms of psychological manipulation, had never been Ivy's lot, but he understood it and the person who used it. That was because he was a Hollow Man just like the man who applied the heated blade to his body. Maybe it was this golden armored knight applying the glowing sword to Ivy's body, but he could, deep in his mind, see the roles reversed. Ivy would ride out the torture and die rather than say a single word about his friends to these shits.

As the heated metal came down on his leg again, he thought that the banality of not having a home was itself an indictment of him. He screamed as sizzling hot steel transferred its energy next to his thigh. He screamed, cursed, and struggled to be away from the blade, but inside he watched the metal hungrily punish him as he knew he deserved punishment. His partner, the quest, Kelle the woman he had vowed to protect was a wall across his soul, but nothing lay beyond the wall. It was all exposed.

"Je vais te tuer, connard!" He screamed. *"Donne m'en plus!"*

The knight hesitated, stepping back from Ivy as he strained against his straps. Screaming rage was not the normal reaction he was used to from a prisoner. Ivy inwardly smiled. *Here is where I die,* he thought, *yet another Hollow Man.*

The Wizard and the knight were talking to themselves, arguing the meaning of his words, so Ivy turned his attention to the crowd. He saw the villagers had been crowded to the edge of the clearing by soldiers. The village elders were standing stoically, like torture was not new to them, but there was glances to the sides as each reassured the other that they had done the right thing. Then, he turned to another form, the girl from the meal who had served him food and drink. She was hiding in the deep shadows of the trees, trying to break free from restraining hands. Others also looked ready to brook the weapons of the soldiers to protest the torture. They were like rabbits snapping at a farmer's dogs as the farmer clears his traps of unlucky game animals. Fierce in their impotence, angry in their helpless protest.

The knight came up and switched languages from the haughty tone of superiority to the intimate form of the lowland speech. "Call out to this Kelle woman." The glowing blade was between them, its heat radiating the air. "You are a cog. A red shirt, I am told. What are you defending? Scream her name. The Wizard can use that to trick her, he assures me, and I believe him." The blade swung closer to Ivy's stomach. "Soon, I will start burning you in ways that the healers cannot repair. Terrible ways. The only thing standing between you and that is that we do not need an incoherent babble. We need you to say her name loudly!" The blade came down with a hiss.

Ivy screamed all right, but he thought of watching Kelle bathe in the stream at a little farm. He thought of Rains-a-Lot suddenly playing hopscotch in some Georgia town with three girls on some long-forgotten mission. He thought of the parlor of a house in Hue where he met Chantal in the steaming summer rains. He pictured his mother on the veranda of the Place d' Armes in Casablanca as the Muezzin, crooning his beautiful calls, yelled forth across the city, *"'a-hadu 'anna Muḥammadan rasūlu Llāh!"*

The steel came away, and he yelled the Arabic prayer over and over. It made him smile to think that for the first time he had ever call on God, he had called on it in the beautiful tones that had so enchanted him as a youth. Ivy felt inside the Hollow Place that existed inside of his own soul, and he embraced it.

"You, who they call Lupufocu. You who is Ronceville. Hear my benediction now as you end my life. You are weakness, but here I declare my allegiance. I am a Frenchman who shall never see France again. I am the oath-bound brother of Rains-a-Lot, and my deepest love is a woman whose name I will not say here. I am no longer a Hollow Man. I am the filled man. God and the gods can watch me die. I will speak no more words to you."

He remembered what someone had said to him—in Virdea, oaths matter. They are real things that carry with them strength and magic. Heroes carry a reputation with them based on the oaths they make; the oaths they keep increase that reputation. He looked now not at his torturers who were arguing furiously about how to bend their captive to their will but at the darkened forest and the scared villagers who were to witness his swan song. Over the pain, he started to yell out loud a new song,

Allons, enfants de la patrie,
Le jour de gloire est arrivé!
Contre nous de la tyrannie
L'étendard sanglant est levé!
Entendez-vous, dans les campagnes
Mugir ces féroces soldats?
Ils viennent jusque dans nos bras
Égorger nos fils, nos compagnes!

In the end, there was no home to go to; he had to make one up. He shut his eyes as the glowing metal came down again, and he was standing in a field with Kelle. She was regarding a Vietnamese baby that lay swaddled before her fondly. Behind her was Rains-a-Lot and a dark-skinned woman in a purple dress. Her beautiful hair and skin were perfectly turned out. He looked behind himself and saw a cabin made of wood surrounded by sunflowers, which stood on a hill of rolling grain, red, cox-combed, proud stalks of Quinoa and shifting golden-topped wheat. Milk cows stood obediently in a shed, their cheeses filling an unseen cave, while sheep stood farther out, their wool glowing finely in the summer sun. Across the field a man in an odd suit, his body made of black smoke. He calmly said in a British accent, "Consider the ravens."

Ivy opened his eyes and said, "Have you considered the ravens?"

The metal was about to come down on his cheeks, but the Wizard yelled, "Wait!"

"Waiting is for cowards," Lupufocu said. "Here we get to his meat, yet 'wait' you yell. You are an old woman."

The Wizard said, "Before you maim his ability to talk, listen to what he can say." He removed his cowboy hat, showing his bald head with its numerous tattoos. "Speak, doomed one."

"A smart man might take a second to consider the ravens." It was all he could do to croak the words, but Ivy chuckled over the cleverness of it all.

Lupufocu growled, "And that is worth stopping our fun?"

"Are you an idiot?" the Wizard asked. Behind Lupufocu, his men grew angry at the insult of their lord. Ivy laughed again, if only to block the agony that threatened to overtake him.

The Wizard turned around and around. "Where did the damn ravens go?"

Lupufocu said, "Who cares?"

From the darkness of the woods, a pair of startling lights came on and a deep, rumbling, animal noise could be heard. A song began to play from the car's speakers: "Gimme Shelter."

Then, with a roar, a great purple steel beast burst forth. It moved in an odd way, its tires squealing, the rear of the automobile fishtailing. Despite not hitting any soldiers directly, they began to fall down like 10-pins, swept from their feet by some invisible force. Ivy closed his eyes, almost losing consciousness in his agony, then opened them as he felt someone dragging him from the clearing. It was the young woman Maricia using all of her strength to pull him into a clump of trees.

The music twanged from the Chevy as Ivy's eyes fell on one tableaux after another, his pained mind over-cranking the scenes like some slow-motion fantasy. Rains-a-Lot, armed with a bolt-action rifle he used more like a club than a gun, was advancing through armored men as they tried to regain their feet, cutting them down if they stood, glowing golden in invincible light. Kelle, hands bursting with red lightning, screaming unheard curses, followed Rains-a-Lot, stopping thrown spears in midair to keep them from impacting the Lakota. The Chevy switched gears and made an unnatural bootlegger reverse, then accelerated at Lupufocu, missing him by inches, but again reversing. Lupufocu brought his sword up to strike at the mechanical demon, mowing down his soldiers, but as the 1957 Chevy passed him a second time, he inexplicably ripped into two pieces.

It was now the Wizard named Judius Ronceville facing Kelle, Rains-a-Lot, the Troubadour, and a Purple 1957 Chevy containing the soul of Mamma LeDeoux across a wooded glade, a huge fire, and guttering torches casting flickering light across the scene, the eerie music notes emanating from the mechanical beast. Ivy felt his bindings loosed, then he could tell someone had draped his shoulder harness on his naked form. He looked at his benefactor. It was indeed Maricia of Fisk. Her eyes were clouded in tears, and she was shivering. Ivy touched her cheek in compassion and said, "My darling, do not weep."

She cried harder, "They ruined you."

He looked down at his naked form. Indeed, he was a mass of blistered skin and angry red pustules. He touched her head again and said, "I live." He then marched up to stand with his fellow travelers. He did not have a home in the past tense. His home was with the people who would rescue him from doom and damnation without a thought.

Even naked and crippled, it clothed him in scintillating robes of warmth.

Ivy pulled his Browning and brass checked it. Then, he threw the harness into the Chevy. Like the rest of the universe, he moved in slow motion, but the world seemed to be paused for his benefit. He looked in at the Troubadour who was removing a cable from the back of the Chevy's bumper, the invisible cause of the dying soldiers. With a flash of a smile, the Troubadour nodded at him, then scampered back into the automobile and began to rev the Chevy's engines. The girl helped Ivy limp to where Rains-a-Lot and Kelle stood. Kelle glanced at him while he approached.

"Jesus, I did not think you were the full-frontal type. Think we can get Ewan McGregor to play you in the movie? He might need a prosthetic though." She notably looked at her comrade's genitals to avoid looking at his horrible burns and marks of torture.

Ivy stumbled a little then rose up again. "Only if we can get Brigitte Helm to play you."

"I am more of a Joanna Gaskell type." Kelle turned back to the Wizard. "Judius, you are fucking scum."

"I would not have to do this if you would listen to reason." Judius responded. The Wizard was on the edge of fury.

Ivy said, "So you dated this guy?"

"I did," Kelle said from the corner of her mouth.

"He is, how you say, a dickflute." Ivy felt his scarred burns screaming at him.

"Dick, that is appropriate." Kelle faced the Wizard. "There is no outcome here where I end up with you, Judius. You have chased me too far."

The Wizard stepped forward. "I love you."

Rains-a-Lot scoffed. Kelle said over her shoulder, "I was young."

Silence from Rains-a-Lot. Silence that said a lot.

"He had a huge palace," she said again.

More silence, only the sound of a muted Rolling Stones song could be heard.

"ENOUGH!" The Wizard yelled as the Troubadour turned up the song and jammed the Chevy into gear.

Kelle did a turn like a discus thrower and tossed a lightning bolt at the Wizard. He reflected it into space and shot a bolt of force back, knocking Kelle off her feet. Ivy hobbled into a painful charge, pistol extended before him, taking aim and firing until his magazine was dry. The Wizard raised his hand and stopped the bullets, which turned and raced back at Ivy, one penetrating his left bicep. Then, the Chevy caught the Wizard on the hip, tossing him to the ground.

The Wizard recovered just in time to catch Rains-a-Lot's rifle in the side of his head. He stood and began an intense exchange of blows and parries before the Chevy again swept the Wizard into the air, landing him in a heap on the ground. Kelle was up, a Whitney Wolverine pistol pulled from concealment, shooting it at the fey wizard. Her shots missed, but Rains-a-Lot was able to hit him in the gut with the rifle butt. The butt bent under the force of the blow and the Wizard cast a spell that froze Rains-a-Lot. Before he could do worse, Ivy hit him with a branch of wood retrieved from the ground.

The Wizard grabbed Ivy by the neck and started to squeeze with magical force when the Chevy returned, running over Judius's leg, forcing a horrible scream from his lips. He turned, dropping Ivy, his forehead pressing into the muzzle of Rains-a-Lot's paratrooper rifle. Rains-a-Lot pulled the trigger, but the Wizard apported away in a puff of orange smoke.

AN ARMY OF ROGUES

DATE: 4TH DAY OF THE RAM, 3684
LOCATION: CLAYTON FISK, VIRDEA

They had been here just a day before; it was infuriating. Shibbula had chosen, unlike his fellow riders, to form an army of rogues and mercenaries rather than return to the city-state, but at least one of his competitors that returned had moved quicker than him. His body, cut in two, lay before him.

Lord Shibbula was hardly recognizable as a lord or a great warrior. Gone was his golden armor and great warhorse. In its place was a leather jerkin over which had been hung a mail shirt. His main weapon now was an iron chain wrapped around his waist. At the end, he had locked a rusty padlock. His army, too, was unique in the annals of Carkoza. Four hundred and twenty-one men of low breeding had heeded his brazen horn call for those who could wield a blade and asked no questions of conscious.

A group burst into the clearing, prodding and pushing a second group before them. Banji Moon, his lead scout, stopped before him and gave him a slattern's salute. "Captain, the Rogues found this lot drunk and aslumber in the village. Someone urged high spirits into them."

Shibbula looked them over. Much like his own Twenty-Score-Rogues, they were the dregs of the cup of wine upset by the turmoil caused by the passing king and the slaughter of the professional army. Each was a mote of jealousy, hate, and fear, rolled into flesh by uncaring gods and tossed onto the roiling sea. He could expend such men like bolts in a crossbow and no one would possibly care, but this did not make them ideal recruits. “Who is your leader?”

A pained man stepped forward. He was dressed in leathers and had a horse’s mane hanging from his shoulder. “You are?” Shibbula asked.

The man tried the route of defiance. “I am Glabius, Hetman of the brother of the Horse Lords. You had best modify your tone with me.”

Wearily, Shibbula crooked his finger. “So much is a life worth,” he said as Banji Moon pushed a spike through the man’s chest from the back. Sputtering blood, Glabius fell across the mutilated body of Lupufocu and coughed himself to death as everyone in the glade watched. When the play had reached its final act, Shibbula looked up and said, “Who is your leader?”

Cautiously, a second man stepped forward. He was thinner than most of the Hetman, with coarse blond hair and lighter skin. “Fingerty Foe, my lord.”

“Any relation to the Warriors of Foe?”

“Hammerfoe is my sister, but I am not accepted as a member of the clan.” He was a strong man, or so Shibbula thought, but he could imagine it being hard to live up to the Foe clan expectations.

“And the reason for this?” Shibbula asked.

“I was declared Trickster by the Queen of Fire and Ice,” he sounded defiant.

“No doubt you were innocent,” Shibbula scoffed cruelly.

Fingerty Foe stood up taller and more defiant, “As a matter of fact, I am and was.”

'The Queen is contrary," said the armored lord.

"So they say, My Lord."

"Where are the villagers?" asked Shibbula.

Fingerty Foe growled, "Absconded with our payment."

Shibbula turned and stared with great interest. "Payment for what?"

"Sugar pumpkins, to make alcohol." Fingerty sounded unsure, almost embarrassed at the answer.

Shibbula lifted his head and let the breeze flow through his hair. Helmets were so constricting that it was liberating to stand without rigid armor around his body. "What was the alcohol for?"

"To drive their mechanical beast forward."

Fuel. Any horse driven long and carrying a rider needed grain; grass or weak fodder would not do.

"Your lot are enlisted into my company. Gather supplies and weapons, we move in the morning."

CAMPFIRE TALES

DATE: 11TH DAY OF THE RAM, 3684
LOCATION: THE CASSOCK FENS, VIRDEA

Rains-a-Lot's vision expanded as he traveled across Virdea. He had forgotten how far a warrior attuned to magic could see across the landscape. He could see his boss chasing him from one hiding place to another, dedication blazing in his heart. He could see the Wizard with his ill-famed armies racing with the final dregs of the Yellow Kingdom for his place at the buzzard's banquet. He could feel the attention of the ravens as they scouted for the travelers, carried messages to and from the Great Meadows, and turned the flight of Kelle and her friends into an epic adventure.

He could also see what the constant flight was doing to their group. Surprisingly, it was physical pain that was replacing the emotional pain each started with. Kelle, the woman who wore loud dresses as if to say, "I am here," to a world that rejected her, now was the calm and confident leader of their band. She no longer looked at Ivy when laying out their next day's movement or assumed an inferior stance to the Troubadour. Now, she was like some diminutive field marshal in her demeanor, respectful but positive on what she intended to do.

Ivy had refused to be left at a village with a shaman to treat his horrible torture, but despite that he almost seemed to have been saved by the horror of his experience. During the day, he was all duty, but now and again, he would talk about things in his past. He mentioned Korea, and the Street Without Joy, and the black soldiers he had fought alongside in France.

He had also fallen into a strange chaste experience with Kelle. They would, when no one was looking, hold hands and look at the stars. Rains-a-Lot was not sure they kissed at all, but they did seem every bit as intense as a full-blown bedding. He had seen it on the plains when lust boiled over to something else, a primal longing to be in the orbit of another person, perhaps held back by an understanding that death stood at the back of each sunset.

Rains-a-Lot's introspection was growing as well. They were maybe days away from the Emerald City, and he could feel that the raw, painful underside of his scalp was cooling each day. He woke each morning and saw people and had to remember they were not of his tribe. He was thinking the day would come when he forgot to remember this, and each member of the coterie became just another brother or sister of the Lakota to him.

Then there was the mother. Her frenetic attempts to mother and protect had smoothed into a soft feeling of ease. She reminded Rains-a-Lot of his own stepmother, Blue Flower. She insisted on the camp, and her own metal chassis were kept spotless, but in return, she protected each of the travelers, supporting them in times of pain, celebrating them in times of victory, never forgetting she was a part of the group.

What of the Troubadour? Rains-a-Lot approached the young, handsome man as he sat under a rain tarp, away from the temporary shelter they had built by a crackling fire. Amazingly a giant raven sat next to him, picking at bits of fresh rabbits they had traded for in the last village.

"I feel thin, Rains-a-Lot."

Rains-a-Lot nodded and sat down. He reached over to a pack and took out some parched corn and a bota of water. The group was camped in a glade by an old temple to Tempester, its statues tumbled and walls caved in, but with a small, sweet artesian well blossoming up through a small cenote. They had broken out of the red-soiled plains and into the lowlands just a few days before, and now we're slowly traveling the very end of the Yellow King's Highway. The glade that held the temple was surrounded by a riot of vegetation, including tangled, black forests of live oak, sudden sand spits filled with pines and Cypress, and amazing spider banyan dressed with the colorful reds of great figs hanging pregnant with luscious, sweet, yellow fruit.

As they had entered the Ram, the monsoons started, and now each day was divided into period when it was dry enough to travel on the corduroyed trade roads, and periods, sometimes 30 or 40 hours long, when all that could be accomplished was to find dry ground and wait for the storms to end. Rains-a-Lot looked at the Troubadour. He looked thin, almost transparent. The Troubadour looked back. "Do you suppose Ivy likes this weather because of Vietnam?"

Rains-a-Lot shrugged. Ivy liked rain, but it was despite Vietnam rather than because of it. The raven squawked. Rains-a-Lot regarded it and then looked up at the Troubadour for a translation.

"The raven reminds me I have entered a deal. I must represent Kelle and your lot before the Queen of Fire and Ice." He looked at the fire across the clearing where Ivy and Kelle sat huddled together. The Frenchman's hand gently stroked Kelle's neck, while she stared at the ground. "Only I am fading so fast. I see an apartment. A bath tub. Inescapable purpose."

The raven danced a few steps then opened its wings for a second. Rains-a-Lot caught the Troubadour's eye and stared at him. The Troubadour replied by saying, "Duty and loss, I understand what you are saying. Have you heard the story of the Red Princess?"

Rains-a-Lot shook his head.

"The Oldari split into three groups at the dawn of the world. The Havenites retreated to the great magical forests where they changed themselves. They created a trick where an Oldari of uncommon mental power would have red hair. For some reason, these Oldari are always female, and they are allowed to become the highest rulers of their land, but only after proving themselves.

"The current Queen had a daughter, but she disguised her hair with magic to make it red so they might form a dynasty. Despite this, she could not win the votes of council who knew the Queen's daughter was not worthy to replace the old Queen. They elevated instead a nobody from the border guards. That nobody, though, was overthrown and sold into slavery.

"It was in slavery that she was found by the Darkfather. He helped her escape, taught her magic, protected her from an evil wizard who had enslaved her, and brought to almost to a place of safety. The Darkfather, though, was touched by hubris. He wanted the princess for himself, but he was undead and she was fey, and it could never happen. When he realized this, he threw himself into a battle to make him worthy of her love and disappeared just as he defeated the evil wizard.

"The princess threw herself into her magic, but the loss of a love that could never be changed her. She grew hard and cold."

Rains-a-lot nodded. Ivy had things to solve in his mind. He had taken the first step, but his heart was still buried in the jungles of Asia. The raven suddenly started squawking in alarm. Rains-a-Lot turned.

The Troubadour was no longer there. He was no longer thin, but gone from reality. Rains-a-Lot looked up at the raven and wondered who was in that shell-of-feathers. It seemed at each pathway the ravens stood to help them. They found them places to camp. They helped them avoid ambush. Food and water came to their hands through the ravens. In a mundane sense, the group might have failed long ago if they had not had the services of these birds.

In his youth, Rains-a-Lot had been taught about the spirits of the plains, the great powers that dispensed wisdom and helped guide the people away from starvation and to plenty and spiritual fulfillment. Only most of the spirits of the plains were tied to geographical locations and needed to be traveled to for their help. The spiritual force in the birds traveled with them, like a portable place of magic.

Rains-a-Lot got up and walked into the woods, past the broken walls of the temple, over the rain swollen brook, and into a glen where will-o-wisps flitted in graceful patterns of magical dance. He took off his jeans, his leather jacket, his shirt, and his top hat. He removed his gun belt and his boots. Then naked, he stood and let the rain fall over him.

He remembered Old Man, who had entered the Tornado at Mission Wells with him after they had killed Richard Mangerer and the Fifth Street Kid, the two men most responsible for the slaughter at Pine Ridge. The Old Man had been broken by Wounded Knee, the dead in the snow, the savage delight the soldiers took in having slaughtered starving Lakota. And he had felt that accusation that it was his own fault as well. Time spent learning white man's law, the Old Man had said, was time he could have been learning the dance.

In the terrible rain, his voice sang up, incanting the spell of power for the dance, then he began to do the shuffling steps of power. The song words, when done right, were meaningless. This was why the anthropologists never could make sense of what was being said. The dance steps used by the shaman had no set pattern. The power in the words and the dance was that each dancer chose the next word and the next step based upon the shape of the universe that was directly in front of them, not by any wrote memory of uniformity. The only rule was that every 13th step had to be placed down at a break in the musical chanting, the sign that the dancer knew the universe and was willing to confirm, if only for a single step, their place in it.

As he began dancing and chanting, he felt the presence of two others in the rain-inundated glade. The first was a dark figure in an impeccable suit holding an umbrella with hands, heel, and a head made of dark industrial smoke. The second was a nude African woman. They each had picked up the ghost dance and were dancing with him.

"Thriller was written to the basic beat of the ghost dance," the smoking man said, lifting his free arm up like a mantis and turning back and forth. "I sensed the Troubadour, but now he is gone."

Rains-a-Lot was innately fearful of magical beings appearing in human form. If they appeared as animals, they had rules that had to be followed. As humans though, there was no telling what they could do and no way to predict the outcome of any encounter. Still, this was why he was dancing. The dance was above all, the dance of truth.

The smoking man said, "Ah, the Lakota never figured out that one. Wovoka sold them on ancestors walking forth to do battle with the whites, never knowing that this was exactly what would happen, and not being creative enough to see that the battle was more metaphorical and could be lost." The man swung his arm and umbrella up to one side, then the other, lifting his leg in the air at the same time.

Rains-a-Lot continued his dance, looking occasionally at the smoking man, and more often, at the beautiful black woman dancing silently. She looked at him and he said, "Violet LeDeoux." Then he looked down and continued his dance.

The dance continued for a while, then the smoking man broke the silence again. "The dance was designed to attract the attention of a spirit, who would then be compelled to show the people who were dancers of truth, and those dancers could use that truth to resist tyranny. The sorcerer you killed was trying to use the truth of the dance to create a crack in time, where power, real temporal power, can shift hands, forming a new world order. Sadly, the dancers were pawns, nothing more. Old Man, in recruiting you, gave you a sense of debt. The truth is, you would have died in the snow with the rest of the dancers, and nothing would have changed, except some evil men might have succeeded, where they otherwise failed."

Rains-a-Lot missed a step. The ghost dance faded, and he was left standing alone in a grotto, naked, and covered in rain. He looked up in the tree and saw that the raven had followed him here. In a few steps, he reached into his clothing and drew his pistol, the weapon he had taken from Thomas Jackson so long ago. He took careful aim at the raven, spirit or flesh, that was in some ways guiding their fate the same way that the spirits were. Then he felt a purple haze draw around him, an embracing feeling of love that he had not felt in years. The raven took no move to save itself, it only stared at him and blinked, as if being taken out of the story was just another page to confound the reader.

Rains-a-Lot lowered his pistol and started to get dressed.

NELSON MCKEEBY

DATE: JUNE 24, 2018
LOCATION: MARICOPA COUNTY, ARIZONA

I was fading in and out of reality. First, I was soaring with my brothers and sisters as we scouted the Dead Lands for the Travelers. Then, I was curled up on the ground being beaten with collapsible batons while someone yelled, "Hold the mutherfucker still." Then, I was feasting on the entrails of a deer, feeling the sweet sense of a filled stomach as it brought warmth to my entire body. I was then looking into a flashlight while a woman in a uniform yelled at me, "What have you taken? What are you on?"

I was asleep for a while, dreaming of burning bodies in a field in Iowa, about the girl who I could not save from CPR, about the dead walking at me, my parents torn apart from cancer, my Mexican friends who died while traveling the far winds. So much lost, never to come home, stories never to be told unless I told them. My own obsession that the dead could speak only if I wrote them mouths.

I awoke under harsh fluorescents. A man said next to me, "You have to make a plea!" I was dehydrated and felt the skin hanging on me. A day or two unconscious from having a seizure had passed. My back was a curlicue of pane where I had been repeatedly dumped onto hard surfaces. When the powers that be think an epileptic is a drunk or a druggie, they take it out not in outright torture, but in disdain that results in numerous small injuries to places that are otherwise hard to hurt.

"For what?" I croaked.

"Mister Campheche, your client is trying my good humor." I squinted through the dreadful light of the fluorescent lamps. The woman in the black robes had no apparent humor, as much as I was qualified to tell. Her mouth was a mobile slash that hid perfectly white teeth; the type of teeth rich people could afford. She wore light makeup that said she was professional, but not vain, but her cheeks were ruddy red suppressing the fury of a sudden outbreak of anger. I looked over at the man called Mister Campheche. He was a cowed, brittle person, sweating in an ill-sized sports coat and a load of futility. His skin was a gray color, as if the walls of this courtroom had stained his natural human tan or brown into a lifeless dun that rejected the concept of human blood flowing through corpuscles. As I looked at what must be my lawyer, I felt the powerful hands of authority wrench my head to stare at the judge. In my ear, he said, "Pay respectful attention or you will lose a kidney." That would be a bailiff.

I faded for a second, then returned.

"Make a plea!" my lawyer said.

I tried to stand up straight and failed. Instead, I was like a puffy mound of hay swaying in the breeze of August. Everyone leaned forward to hear what I would say, like they were all tied to my tongue by puppet strings. "Not guilty," I croaked. What else could I say, I did not know what I was charged with.

The man next to me, the woman in the judge's robe, a man at an opposite desk standing with a precisely attired deputy sheriff, and the gorilla behind me all moaned. I had definitely said the wrong thing.

"Let me explain one more time Mr. McKeeby your options, and then we will try this again. Due to the extreme stupidity of the Arizona law system, Maricopa County cannot use its laws that prevent public intoxication against you. It is perfectly legal for you to have consumed so much of an unknown narcotic that you were physically endangered. For that reason, you have been charged with disorderly conduct, which is disturbing the peace for the layman, a crime of which you cannot defend yourself from being declared guilty. Let's be clear, you were found highly intoxicated shaking in the street, you refused orders to get up and leave, when officers tried to stop you from making a scene, you slapped and punched them. You failed to give your name and provide identification to the officers, and you made disturbing sounds forcing the officers to repeatedly deploy a taser and a baton, for which those officers now must spend a week off the streets at the expense of the city, and possibly months in city-paid counseling to get over. This is a class one misdemeanor on your part, and if I had my way would be a felony."

"I have epilepsy," I croaked. I had been fading as each seizure dragged more of me from myself.

"You interrupted me, and you have perjured yourself in court. Provide proof you have epilepsy."

"Ah, judge," my lawyer said cautiously, "the police took a considerable amount of medical alert jewelry from my client."

"Did they take a certified letter from an Arizona neurologist stating he was not only an epileptic, but not taking narcotics at the time of his arrest?"

"No, Your Honor." The lawyer was confused. "I am not sure a doctor would write a letter predicting my client's drug use status once he leaves a medical exam room."

"Good, now shut up, Mr. Campheche. Mr. McKeeby, you have been charged with a serious misdemeanor, but I am offering leniency. Plead guilty, and I will remand you to home custody, and treatment paid for by the state, as long as you give up your narcotics to the treatment center. Plead innocent, and I will declare you guilty and send you down for 60 days. Now, one last time, make a plea."

I looked over at the court reporter. She was young, maybe 25, and was resting her hands, not having recorded the judge's previous comments. She smiled at me sweetly, round face and dark complexion backed by some hidden intelligence. I opened my mouth, and she poised her hands. "Not guilty."

I did not hear the rest because I passed out when the bailiff planted my head on the defense table.

I must have been under another day as I awoke delirious for water and on the south side of dehydration. I was wearing a suicide proof potato sack prison garment. There was a deputy sitting outside of my cell. When she saw I was awake, she yelled down the silent and empty block, "He's up!"

A big sergeant came down the walkway, red faced from days on end in the sun. He took the chair, sat down in front of my cell, and sent the younger deputy away. From inside of a bag of Chick-Fil-a, he pulled a water bottle. I greedily grabbed it and sucked it down in a single long swallow. The sergeant frowned and yelled down the hall, "Get me a big bottle of water!" The deputy returned with a gallon jug, which would not pass through the cell bars, but which the sergeant poured neatly, without spilling a drop, into the smaller water bottle, as long as I asked for more.

After most of the gallon had run down my gullet, I stopped drinking and held the bottle to my head, and then found I was being offered a pair of chicken sandwiches. Were these the same guys who I assumed beat my ass? I ate the sandwich and watched as the sergeant pulled a metal badge from his pocket. It was a deputy's badge that said, "Richland County Sheriff's Department." On a rocker, it said, "Richland 919R."

"Is this yours?" The guard looked abashed, like he had been caught peeing on the courthouse steps by his father.

"Yes," I said.

"The boys did not know," he said with a guilty glance to the door. By the boys, he meant the men who had beaten my ass when I came in and who made sure that each judicial pronouncement was supported by a physical dimension.

I nodded. "I need my epilepsy medicine."

The sergeant looked cloudy and glanced behind himself. "The department will only allow you to have Dilantin."

"I am allergic to Dilantin," I said. And he could not understand the hell I would face from taking it, my skin blistering and dying before my eyes, my last days in agony from a rare allergic reaction that happened with nearly all of the epilepsy medicines.

"I know. We read your records. You do not have a lot of time left," he said this while looking down at my shoeless feet.

"Really?" I stared at him for a second then said, "That is really sad to hear. Too bad I will be spending part of that time in this place for, what was it, disturbing the peace. Did anyone find any narcotics in my system?"

He looked me in the eyes finally, something concrete to say, "Blood and hair, no. No narcotics, no booze, nothing that could alter your behaviors. Does not matter, disturbing the peace does not require intoxication, and an appeal will take longer than, frankly, I bet you have."

I held up the chicken sandwich. "So what is this, a consolation prize? Ease your conscious by not feeding me green baloney? "

"Hey, I eat that baloney. It's not terrible." He looked like he believed what he said.

I nodded and rolled over in my bunk.

"Look, I am sending a trustee by. Tell them what you want to eat and drink. You want a TV set, or a computer, or some books, whatever you like. The judge does not rescind her rulings, not ever. You are in here for 60 days unless you change your plea," he paused for a second by the cell door, then went down the corridor, his boots echoing off the painted floors.

I fell asleep for a while. It must have been an hour when a trustee came by. He was an older Mexican man with gang tattoos on his face and a happy, serene smile. He shuffled up and said, "Hey there, you want to make some food orders with me?"

I sat up. "Name's Nelson."

"Rodrigo." He was dressed in yellow prison coveralls with his sleeves rolled up and a hoody tied up around his hips.

I reached my hand out and shook his, "Did I choose the wrong place to get arrested?"

Rodrigo laughed. "Mister, you sure did not."

I goggled at him. He said, "A couple of the deputies, some of the judges, they are rotten, sure, but you think Pinal County is any better? Arpaio was the dumbest dumb-shit that ever lived. That prick never did find out his outdoor jail was like a vacation. And I know 50 guys who got big, secret payoffs for racial profiling. Hell, bad boys were standing in line to get arrested and get their ass beaten by Maricopa because it was the greatest way to earn money since selling crack. Less dangerous also, sell crack and you get your ass beaten all the time, and maybe shot. Now? The current guy is back to crime and punishment and is way smarter than Arpaio. While Arpaio was rolling teenagers and using his people to piss on town folk, the vatos owned the county. Now, they are running scared."

"Really?" I asked.

The older man laughed from deep down inside, "On the grave of Santa Maria." He then said, calming down, "Do you know how many Mexicans voted for the guy?"

I replied, "I have no idea."

"None, Mexicans cannot vote in the United States." He started scribbling on a piece of paper as he chuckled, then slid it to me. The paper said:

> *Change your plea to No Contest. Visit Phoenix Park 'n Swap and talk to Juan Cartier. Do what he says, then go to your drug counseling appointment. Good luck.*

The hand was almost a Spencerian script, very surprising considering the hand's owner. I did what it said and was out on the streets a day later, free as a bird. Or free-ish. I had been shown the door at the squatty brick 4th Avenue complex. My clothing was a bloody ruin, so the jail had given me flip-flops, shorts, and a t-shirt. My money and credentials were handed over in a plastic shaving case, less $542 removed from my pouch to pay the court cost and cost of incarceration. To remain free from arrest and keep my record clear, I had to visit the drug councilor that evening for a checkout, then follow through with the suggested course of treatment. First, though, I had to visit Juan Cartier.

The Uber picked me up at the jail, but it took three calls to get one to not cancel the pickup. I was too tired to fight, so I just leaned my head against the window of the Taurus that finally grabbed my ride. The Uber ended up dropping me at Gateway several blocks from the real terminus of the ride. I thanked him and, in my head, blessed the world that allowed people to earn a living driving people about. I missed cabbies and their feral knowledge, but Ubers were more human.

The Park 'n Swap was a frenetic hive of multicolored commerce, people sweating, smiles and avarice on the shopper's faces. I bought slacks, a shirt, slip-on-shoes, suspenders, and a used sports coat. If Mister Cellophane got a job as a used car salesman, he would have looked a lot like me—an ill-fitted vagabond worn down by dust and miles. I then looked up Juan Cartier. He turned out to have a small shop at the geographic center of the meet that sold knives.

Most knife stores in the swap meet sell substandard crap knives. Bar steel ground down to a shape, more or less brittle for lack of heat treatments, with flashy handles and edges that would cut paper but were impossible to sharpen again. Juan Cartier's knives were all forged, heat treated, and oil quenched, seax, Bowie, and dagger-shaped weapons made by serious smiths. The prices matched the quality, and it looked like his business was occasional. People with an eye for quality and willingness to pay the right price, the rest bought shit at the adjoining tables.

Cartier was a dark-skinned man with perfect teeth and a smile that could light up a room. His eyes were equally bright, opening wider than was natural and filled with amazement at the world. "Brother, you look like a man who is good with a seax!"

I did not reply, just handed him the paper with the Spencerian script. He said, "Hell man who rolled out the carpet and painted it red!"

"Any thoughts?"

Cartier waved at the vendor next door and then nodded at me. I followed him out to the parking lot. He popped his trunk and then showed me in the palm of his hand an Arizona State Police badge. "You gotta convince that counsellor that you are a dog, and you want the leash, yeah?"

I shrugged, putting my hands in my pocket. He looked around the parking lot then slipped a baggie into my pocket.

"That is cut 'H.' You ever snort?"

I shook my head no.

"About an hour before the appointment, snort down this, then take a shower and burn the baggie." He then handed me a strange metal box. "That is your injection kit, spoon, all the works. Give that to the counselor, tell them you are quitting."

Then, he pulled a big pill bottle. "Valproate. Take four times your normal dose, heroin will drive you to the edge of a seizure."

Hell of a world. That much Valproate could also send my liver into catatonia. It would start with my eyes and skin turning yellow. My abdomen would swell and I would start to vomit. I'd become disoriented and confused, and my joints would start to turn red and hurt. Then, in some ditch between here and some other city, I'd die, thumb outstretched looking for a ride, and my story would never be told. Worse, this story would be over.

I pouched the Valproate. At least I would not have to get a friend to steal me another bottle now; I had enough for maybe three months. I looked through my document bag and found that I had left my traveling gear to the north of the city at the Desert Tortoise Campground, which meant I was in for a nighttime journey.

Hitchhiking was an art I had learned in an earlier life, and the first lesson of hitching was to take public transportation where possible. There was no way my money would hold up if I used Uber, so public transportation, the thumb, and shank's mare were my magic carpet. The swap meet was near the metro-rail, which ran to Central Avenue where the addiction center was located.

Once at the addiction center, I snorted all of the debased heroin I had in the bathroom, probably not the first person who had done that, then used a pen to make some unconvincing needle tracks on my arm. The heroin hit me, and I could understand how a certain weakness of soul could make the drug appealing. It really did take the edge away from a sucky life. I was thankful for paths never followed as I stumbled into my addiction appointment.

An hour later, I was clear of my charges, high off my ass on heroin for the first time in my life, and hitching my way north. I lucked into my first ride to State Road 74. Only it was not luck.

I was dog-tired, and night was falling. Hitching at night was never a good idea. Often, you were picked up by a carload of freshman who offered you a ride and other favors in exchange for illegally purchased booze. Worse was past telling, and hitchhiking is no longer a hobby I indulged in.

So I had not signaled my intention for a ride when a blue 1968 Mustang pulled up in front of me. The driver's door opened, and a woman in a sundress stepped out. Her deep blond, tightly curled hair set off a contrast in the deeply shadowed night with her ebony skin. She was tall, maybe 180 centimeters, and her calf muscles alone, even when partly hidden by engineer's boots, were as big as my shoulder muscles. When she spoke, it was like silk on shamrocks.

"You are Virdea touched, Boss-Eyes."

I walked toward the woman. The idea of riding even a short distance was seductive. Then, she said, "You're not flying it, friend. Look behind you."

I turned and looked. In all of my life, I had never seen myself going through a seizure. I had obviously known it was going to happen as I had crawled off the road and into the gully. My gear was neatly arrayed, and I had set up a sun shelter. "I will probably survive that."

"Yeah, and the cabin changes 'probably' to 'certainly.'"

I suppressed all of my questions. What if I woke up but was not present to reunite with my body? I turned and got into the Mustang. The driver put something in the backseat and then jumped back in.

The car took off, burning a bit of rubber.

"Tess is making chicken pot pie, at least I hope. We set up on the ranch just a couple of months ago." The woman stared at the road, and I stared at her. "Go ahead, check out the merchandise. I do not sling it to your lot, but I don't mind being a bit of wank bait."

I turned away. She really was one of the most beautiful women I had ever seen, but I really had not been staring, except out of the side of my eye, the way most men do. She laughed loudly, "I am just taking the piss, so sorry. Last person I spoke to was that dark-jacketed person who set me and Tess up here, so the chance to talk is wonderful. Tess will want more, being as you are an OK ride and she likes gentlemen as a side dish, but she and I are not at a point where I care to share her, so that is just a friendly warning."

I said, "I think I understand."

"That is the problem with English; no one actually speaks it."

The Mustang rocketed through the night, its 289 engine growling with a thick roar, pushing the 75R14 tires along at 90 plus. The rig's throaty growl sounded as if someone had drilled holes in its muffler, while the tires whistled in the night. No car approached us or tried to overtake us. We were alone in the dark.

With a disorienting fishtail, the car took a side road, kicking up a trail of dirt that glowed in the moonlight. The car lights spread out across the desert. Ahead, a whirl of wind had kicked up more dirt. "Hang on Boss-Eyes," Devone said. They hit the barrier of dirt and the temperature went down 20 degrees in a few seconds while the night went from darkness to sunset. Devone pulled the wheel, and they were on a small dirt track leading to a wooden ranch house. The house had a traditional porch, a tin water house, and a space laid out for gardens, although nothing was growing there. The Mustang came to a slurring stop and Devone leaped out through the open window without bothering to open the door.

On the porch was a woman with blonde-moppy hair and a chiseled face filled with sun freckles. She wore a jeans-style shirt and pants, and had put a Navy Pea Coat over the ensemble. She held a leather ranger's coat sized for Devone. "Who's that?"

Devone said, "He has yet to say, oddly enough."

"Nelson McKeeby," I offered.

The woman looked at me and then said, "Did you go to the Rodehouse?"

"Found him asleep on the side of the road. What's for dinner?"

"Chicken pot pie." She turned and slammed into the house.

Devone looked at me. "Not that happy to see you, it seems."

I followed her into the house. It was frugal to the point of barrenness. A couch with threadbare cushions sat against one wall, with a doorway going off to a bedroom, forming the main room. This room was lit by oil lamps that flickered and guttered in the breeze that seemed to come from every wall. The kitchen was through a door and was lit with gaslights. Warmth poured from that doorway like an ocean current of comfort. Devone directed me in as she went back to the car and returned with a sack. "Care to give this to Tess?"

I grabbed the sack and went into the kitchen. Tess was sitting in the corner of the room, in front of a cooling chicken pot pie and a stack of tin plates. She was smoking a Winston King Size like it had pissed her off, with great draws on the cylinder then purges of smokey air into the atmosphere around her. I silently opened the sack and said, "Devone got you these."

The contents included two cartons of Winstons, a package of autoharp strings, Beefy Boy Tomato seeds, and a packet of Zig-Zags. Tess immediately grabbed up the Zig-Zags and said, "I told her RizLa."

From the other room came a yell, "That or Bugler, Cher."

She tossed the Zig-Zags down and started to open the Winstons. I watched her intently; the Winstons had an unusual packaging, lacking a Surgeon General warning. I looked up and said, "What's going on here?"

"You figure it out from a cigarette carton?"

"Not really."

"You really related to the farmer? You do not look like him."

That came out of nowhere. "What farmer?"

"The one with the pitchfork. The gothic in the Midwest or some such."

"Byron McKeeby and the painting is American Gothic. He was not a farmer. He was a dentist; he just modeled as a farmer. I always thought he looked at bit like Mark Rylance."

"Who is that?"

"Never-mind. Byron was my great uncle." I let myself relax and thought about the odd conversation. Authors are always careful to make sure their characters understand each other with only a limited amount of what I call code guessing. No writer would let their guild fees keep that last confused bit of narrative in their book, but it made me smile to think about. After all, isn't that's how most conversations are? Two people guessing at meaning, trying to come to some understanding?

The woman stood up and went to the cupboard. From it, she took a bottle of Southern Comfort and two small glasses. She poured two fingers in each glass and pushed one to me.

I was not normally a Comfort drinker, but I tilted it back, presuming that in my current status by the side of the road a little alcohol could only aid my ravaged muscles. She drank hers as well. "Been a long time. He thinks you're Virdea Lost, I bet. You ain't that."

"What is Virdea Lost?"

She poured herself another two fingers and topped mine off as well. "Virdea is a magical place. Creativity, remorse, happiness, sadness, and even thought take physical form there. Earth humans transport to that land from time to time, but few stay forever. Most will, at some point, try to return to some time and place on Earth where they can live their happily ever after. Ideally, what they learned in Virdea allows that to happen."

"So, you come back and say this is my time and my place to be of Earth. And you live out your life."

I drank some of the Southern Comfort. "I understand."

"Good. There is a problem, though. People come back, and sometimes they spend the magic, sometimes on worthy causes, sometimes on the most evil things. Then, they are left with no way back. It is like burning your passport and selling state secrets; it is not likely someone will trust you after that, even if you did it for good reasons. You come to Earth and burn all of the magic of Virdea you had, there is no real way to go back."

I nodded. "But some people try."

"They do, and they get caught. Since the ways back to Virdea are often extreme, someone who has spent their magic cannot make it over. And the way they get caught is often hideous." She took a long drag on her cigarette.

"Jesus." I reached over and poured another hit of Comfort.

"No shit. Hideous and perpetual." She took the bottle from me and poured herself another as well.

"Did that happen to you?" I asked.

"Yes. I was an addict. I needed Virdea. It was a drug. I spent what Virdea gave me and ran a physical deficit. Then there came a time when the deficit called, and it left me on the wrong side, on Earth. So I said to myself one more push, triple strength because I thought I could handle it, and off I would go. Only I was stuck in agony; they call that twilight."

"How did you get here, then?" I asked.

"Darkness, an avatar, released me. He built this place of reflection and also gave it to Devone. She also tried to flee to Virdea for different reasons than I had."

I finished my Comfort and declined another glass. Tess put the bottle up, lighting a Winston from the stove. "Pie is going cold, I guess."

I looked at the pie. It still smelled savory and lush, like it was baked by a farm-raised mother from real ingredients that all caused some form of heart disease. Burping Southern Comfort and inhaling Winston smoke; I thought about how dying of epilepsy changed things for some people. Tess broke into my thoughts, "You are Virdea touched, not Virdea Lost. You visit Virdea, but you cannot stay."

"The visits are killing me."

"Drugs almost killed me. I guess booze, also. There is a limit to how much you can find to drink in a cabin in the desert while you're caught in a time loop."

"I think I am addicted to telling the story of Virdea. I have been thinking of quitting it, though. I am reduced to hitchhiking and sleeping in doorways just to speak to someone else who can help me understand the place. When I am having a seizure, usually I become a raven and can witness the story by helping the main characters on their quest."

"You can get arrested in Texas for that I think." She winked at me.

"It certainly complicates the plot. The ethics of the whole damn thing, if I just let the four characters in my story ride into hell, my story will be terrible. They probably will get slaughtered in some dumb way, and my book will end up a disappointment. On the other hand, I need a great battle or some denouement to cap the whole book, or else my readers will revolt. Jesus, it would be like *Lost*, only I won't have a tithe of the audience to hate me."

"Does that matter so much?"

"I do not know. Can I really egg these characters on to the point that they cut each other and hurt each other just for the story? I am a Quaker, for fuck's sake."

Tess reached her hand over and stroked my head. "You may be overthinking this. I mean, how many books have even been read by a publisher? Your best bet is to be yourself, right? Being an intellectual causes all sorts of problems, and that is the book no one writes, the one with all of the answers. You spend so much time with these people in Virdea, and they will never meet you or return your love. Well, baby, that's the whole world, not just Virdea. Quit worrying about this tomorrow, you won't live to see it. Just open your heart and give all you have to helping these people in Virdea who you have fallen in love with, and the audience will fall in love with them, even demanding more, and just let the art flow out, you know? Fuck, anyone can do better than a fucking tinman sans heart, you know what I mean?"

I reached up and held Tess's hand. I looked into her soulful eyes as she stared back into mine, and I knew her inner thoughts, if only for a second. And I realized that she had shared herself a thousand ways by a thousand and still had soul to go around. She was like a female Hale Appleman; all feelings and expressions and inner thoughts covered in a layer of smiles. She kissed me on the head, and I got up.

"Devone, you gotta take Nelson here to the Rodehouse. He has a lot of work to do."

A CONTEMPLATION OF INTER-DIMENSIONAL TRAVEL

by Dr. Kelle Brainerd

There is a point
then a line
then a plane
Fourth is space
Motion is fifth
Direction is sixth.
It gets strange from there
Since we have no organs to detect magnetic
Electrical
or tenth force, gravitational.
After that we find the strong,
then the weak force.
It is in the last dimension where weirdness
sits down,
orders coffee, and screws with your head.
Have you ever tried 13th-dimensional math?
I am sure that Virdea is found there.

THE MUSICIAN AND THE TROUBADOUR

DATE: 1965–1968

There are so many people who have told the story of the Portals that it is not only presumptuous but also naive to think I have more to say on the subject. Jack Rovane, who in Virdea was known as the Troubadour, was the dour, philosophical lead singer and performer who the press and the fans would never understand behind the walls of illusion his magic built. Sadly, I would never meet him in a way that we could speak. We would pass each other in Virdea, but that is hardly a way of getting to know someone. I was, at the time, a raven, and pretty late on my own lifeline. He was known as Troubadour. Early on, his life and mine were endless cases of epochal mischance. He lived in Clearwater as I did for a while, but we missed each other by the smallest of lengths—20 years. His last visit to Florida corresponded with my third birthday, when I was in fact less than five miles from him at one point. Still, any conversation between an autistic three-year old and a musician 26 years older would have been odd.

Randolph Homey brought his guitar and lyrical sense to the Portals. Known as Warsong in Virdea, he never cared for money or fame, and instead spent his magic sparingly on the art, so that when Rovane was a depleted shell, Homey was just starting his career that would last 40 more years.

Pretend that each artist is a candle. And pretend that they have the ability to dip into a big canister of wax once in a while. Jack Rovane would have, like, five wicks twined together. For the average artist, that is a whole lot of light, but his light is like the sun, and he burned himself away before the end of the night he was fighting to stop.

RANDOM ACCESS MEMORY

DATE: 14TH DAY OF THE RAM, 3684
LOCATION: THE RIVER OF VISIONS, VIRDEA

The Wizard of the Obsidian Tower knew that there were other ways to track than to follow. And there was no need to waste his army of henchmen on the search.

Kelle had called his followers Red Shirts, and to please her, he had dressed them in red tunics with strange triangle sigils. She was right that they were to be used, like bolts in a crossbow, but she failed to understand that only a fool wastes bolts.

They had been so good together, the Wizard and Kelle. She was his eager pupil, and in his hundreds of years, having a willing woman in his bed had been a feat. He had remembered when she left him. His seneschal had brought her replacement, a bedwarmer donated to his chamber from one of the local villages. In every way, she was superior. Kelle had small breasts, hardly noticeable in the dark. His bedwarmer's breasts were large and defied gravity. Kelle was tiny, almost girl-like. The bed warmer had moderate hips and a voluptuous posterior.

Yet, for all her superiority, the bedwarmer did not trigger Judius the way Kelle did. There was no conversations of magical theory, of the history of Virdea, or of alchemical practices. The bedwarmer looked down and said, "Yes, Master." That was the extent of her conversation ability.

And sex. Kelle had taught him sex had new meaning when your partner hungered for it. Judius had learned a new word with Kelle, and that was orgasm. He knew men had these. He had several before himself, but he did not know women had the capacity. She would come up to him and put her arms around his shoulders, and close her eyes ducking her head into his chest, then would begin kissing him. Soon, she would have both their clothes off and would yank his very essence out with her body. When his bedwarmer closed her eyes and opened her legs, he wanted to hit her. He could never go back to how sex was supposed to be once he had Kelle.

Now, he had to have her back. He would release her from the thrall of her friends and bring her back to the Obsidian Tower where he would never let her go again. Judius loved her that much.

He walked into the village by the swiftly flowing river rather than flying. A boy stood in the center of the roadstead, so Judius bent to his level and said, "Get the mayor, now."

The boy ran, and slowly the village filed out. Soon, he was in a circle of commoners. The village elders came out wearing keys around their necks and large, plain, straw hats. A boy and a girl were standing by him, in their twenties, each in a shiny gray tunic.

Kelle had railed against this practice. She hated it so much that it would make her scream in rage. She did not understand though, with her Earth ethics, so variable, how this made the contract between rulers and ruled so much easier. The ancient book of submission said that a village owed tithe to its rulers, but that they owed courtesy to any visitor of rank. And that courtesy was meals, water, and the comfort of the lap of a single chosen couple.

This village lived today because it admitted he was the master and that some things were owed to him for restraint. Rapine was not needed if the lower orders accepted their rank. And that saved his time since sex magic was powerful when it was voluntary.

He took the young woman by her hand and walked her into a house. There was a single large bed in the middle of the common room. He let his oni expand into the room. This was not the woman's house. She lived with her family two houses over. This was an older woman's house, a widow. The widow played a recorder, two of which were leaning against a wall. She was finding it hard to keep warm, and the fire was banked higher than needed.

The house had three cats, one of which was actually a small protector spirit and invisible to normals. A clay bowl held a sage smudge, showing the older woman worshipped the traditional gods. His subject and the woman knew each other, but for a small village, they rarely spoke.

Information flowed into the Wizard, and he loved it. And more information would help him track his lost love. He was not ready for the magic, but a small cantrip solved that. He leaned over the village girl and inserted himself in her. She closed her eyes and seemed to act like it was a non-event, no more important than having her hair combed.

Kelle had been a force of nature at sex. She had wanted and given and taught him what sex should be. Then, she took that from him.

He began to cast the spell as he moved in the woman. Sex was such a vile act, pushing and forcing for just a few seconds of release. As the magic built his mind, his body felt the ripening in his stomach. Then, he exploded, and his seed flushed out.

They had been here in this village, and the woman he was attached to had seen them. The purple beast had unleashed the four while villagers appeared from every hovel to greet them. The Wizard smirked as he noticed the village mayor had no keys around his neck, and he did not lead out the traditional young woman and man. They did not consider Kelle and her oddities as worthy of tribute.

He felt a purple thought in his mind questioning his assumptions. Maybe the villagers showed something other than homage. They offered food and were smiling.

The Wizard did not care for smiles. A smile was the facial image you painted on before you eliminated a rival. He never trusted smiles, not ever.

He looked at the four. The Troubadour was lost in time and space. The smallest breath, and he would be gone from the story. It would be interesting to explore him. Where did the Troubadour come from, and how did he attach himself to Kelle and her crusade?

Then, his ethereal vision fixed on Kelle. She was running to help Ivy. The man had been very badly tortured by Lupufocu, and despite his bravado, he was quite seriously damaged. Earth medicine would not save him, his scarred right cheek was brutal, and it was obvious that a toll had been taken on his other reserves.

Mind, Body, Spirit, Soul. Earthlings paid attention to the first two and ignored the damage done to the second two.

But they can learn, came an unbidden purple thought.

The trees around the village had settled with ravens. He had encountered the ridden one, and still did not understand his role in this. They were such tiny morsels, it should be so easy to reach out and stop his heart, but Virdea resisted. Wild creatures were part of the fabric, and you tread lightly with the more advanced magic. He understood that squirrels were part of the canvas, not figures painted on it, and efforts to scrape out the very universe required a great deal more guile than was logical.

They took the wounded man in, and he could see a shimmer of purple.

Purple.

He looped the view into his own mind and entered into an ethereal construct, a virtual space. Standing in it was a breathtaking woman in a purple dress. She was magical, crackling with power. And she was not other/then but now/here. Judius gathered his ethereal self and stood tall in front of her.

"You are foolish to reveal yourself in the dream world to me."

The women replied in English with a heavy accent, like syrup from a sugar tree. "Then, you should deal with me."

The Wizard of the Obsidian Tower concentrated on his target and found the seam, then sent forth energy in the dark. Nothing.

"You cannot affect a body made of metal with your spells."

Judius laughed, "What is your name, haute zombie?"

"Mamma LeDeoux, Macumba of the great compact of the Loa of Petro, Mistress of the Santeria rights."

"And despised, haute zombie. You are the mechanical being."

"I am."

"Ridden like a whore."

"As you say."

"Powerless to stop me."

There was no response. It struck very true.

"Give me Kelle, and I will fashion you a body of flesh, Mistress."

"No golem for me."

"No, a body of a young woman that you may pilot for a year or a hundred years. This one, for example."

The purple woman smiled. "Are you Prometheus to breathe life into clay?"

"You are human underneath, but you forget the great storm I conjured on Earth, a conjuring I completed swimming in an aether as thick as syrup."

"You lost control of that storm."

"But I still made it. Could you free yourself of your metal shell?"

There was no response to that. When wizards fight each other, it is very rarely a fight of the body. The understanding of magical war is that a wizard must only defeat two sides of a three-sided person before facing the final internal kernel. Mind or Spirit could be attacked by words, exposing the Soul to harm.

This was his goal, to dominate the mechanical woman, whose heart was a fuel pump and whose soul was held in an inhuman cage.

"I was a powerful Macumba, but our magic is different, we guide, nurture, protect. We are the mothers of a flock."

The Wizard laughed. "Then why do the so powerful Loa, the beings of the half-world, not free you from your iron mask?"

Again, no answer. "You wear your sin in the form of purple steel. What did you do?"

"I translated Jose Gaspar to immortality through the charm of riding."

The Wizard laughed again. "Ohh, I am surprised you were not punished harder!"

"Into a hematite necklace. I was recycled into a car."

"And Gaspar, what thanks did he give you?"

"A mother demands no thanks of her lover or her children."

The Wizard laughed even more.

"I would not laugh."

"Why not?"

There was a wave of purple confidence. "The mighty Wizard chasing a woman through Virdea, like there are not dozens who would be your slave for a taste of power. In your idiocy, you are her slave, do you not realize?"

"Shut up."

"I sense the Seer's touch on you. She has blinded you as well. Do not tell me you are so weak that an ancient sorcerous can derail your powers. What has she hidden from you?"

"What is between the Seer and I is not between you and I, golem."

"Oh, so now you claim I am golem. I claim you are blinded by the Seer, blinded by the weakness you show, and now blinded by me."

Too late, the Wizard realized that Mamma LeDeoux had cast a spell on him. It was a spell of blinding, making her invisible to his magical searches. He screamed but did not scream too hard. He had cast a spell as well. In her mind, Mamma LeDeoux had revealed their plan. They had gambled all on the benevolence of the Queen of Fire and Ice, which meant he knew right where they were going, and what they planned to do.

RODEHOUSE

DATE: JUNE 29, 2018
LOCATION: SOMEWHERE IN NEVADA

The blinking sign said, “Rodehouse.” I had to look at it twice to make sure. I have always felt the world spends too much time fighting over small spelling and grammar errors.

The Mustang squealed off. Devone had not been happy about taking me to the bar hundreds of miles away. She had to be back by what she called “curfew.” As I was getting out of the car she said, “If you start to wake up, lay down. It will make things easier. And don’t touch any lengths of wire.” She barely waited for me to get out of the car before tearing away.

The Rodehouse was a honky-tonk out of time. Cars, horses, carts, and stranger bits, and pieces of machinery were lined up in a busy parking field, like time was straining samples of every conveyance used by mankind and depositing them here in the asshole of Nevada as a museum exhibit.

The otherworldly feeling of being transported to another dimension was like waking up and finding yourself forced to live life on the set of Streets of Fire. The bar was throbbing with an impossible beat, a syncopation of three music styles. Beside me, a sign said,

"Don't Piss on the Sidewalk." It was buzzing loudly from reflected sound.

Two girls in Flock of Seagulls haircuts walked past.

I lurched up to the door. A petite dark-skinned woman, looking a lot like Marion Ramsey, sat on a stool. She said, "Forty Tolars."

"Tolars?" I asked.

"Slovenian money printed between 1991 and 2007." She looked up and said, "Put your arm out."

I rolled up my sleeve and did as I was told. She scanned my arm with an ultraviolet wand. "Well, you are touched. You never heard of Tolars?"

"Should I have?"

"I should think so. Can't make a transaction without them."

"I was at the Colony; they do not use Tolars."

"Those rustics? Why should they, being on a commune? Ok, so you are a new fish." She picked up a phone and quietly talked into it. When she hung up, she said, "Go in and immediately go to the office. There is a sign. They will sort you. And don't touch any lengths of wire or pipes when you are in there."

I did as I was told. Inside, there was a bar filled with the most diverse group of people I had ever seen. It was as if a Comicon cosplay party had been stuffed into the set of Al Swearengen's Gem Saloon. The big difference was that in a cosplay party, everyone is standing on the front of their feet, trying their best to push their lovingly crafted costumes forward to be seen in the best light. Here, people just wore their clothing without a second thought. In fact, if this lot were judged as cosplayers in a contest, many would have lost. There were in any number of costumes with odd intrusions from different periods and times. Not one was quite authentic. A woman in a Roman toga virilis had a Vostok watch, while another woman in a flapper dress sported iPhone ear buds dangling from her shoulders. If you have ever imagined chain mail would not go with jeans, you would find yourself wrong; several people had serviceable mail accessories and well-made American blue jeans.

I was surprised that non-humans had their place in the bar. I had no idea that the Oldar, what we call Elves on Earth, or the Dwarrow, also known as the Stonekind (or in a vulgar way, Dwarves), existed on Earth at all. I thought I saw the rugged, intelligent jaw line of a Suege, but it turned out to be Peter Dinklage. I nodded at him, but then remembered I only knew him as an actor and not personally. He nodded back though, which was nice.

I have a theory that most places in Virdea, and most people who are refugees from that land, can basically be described by which Game of Thrones cast member they look like. As I walked, I tried to make it a game, saying hello with a nod to Indira Varma, who I felt somehow should be in the company of a Roman officer, and John Bradley, who was the one guy I wanted to have beer with. Then, I saw a Nikolaj Coster-Waldau look-alike walking with a man who could have played Stephen Henderson if the actor needed a stand in, and my brain started to trip out. The room spun, and I hit the floor.

I wake up in an office with a woman staring at me. She did not look like any actress I knew, so I created a new visual file in the cerebral cortex and, looking at the name-tag she was wearing, filed her face under "Wandira Viking, Ph.D."

I looked at the woman and said, "I think I passed out."

She smiled, and the way she did that told me it was an alien facial move. "Technically, you passed in. You arrived on our doorstep, according to the doorkeep, being driven by someone who was Virdea Lost. That means in a fixed cycle of time space or, if you want, out of phase with reality. They can visit here sometimes, but it is not common and somewhat dangerous. You were in the same state of lost time. However, you appear to have reentered phase time. Visiting this club requires one to have knowledge of or have visited Virdea, which your status would argue you have. You puzzled me, though."

"Past tense?" I asked.

She laughed wanly and said, "I meant to say it was essential I know how a Virdea Lost

can become found so to speak. Then, I asked an expert."

She motioned to the back of her office, and for the first time, I noticed a large shadow with a bowler hat. "You are Darkness," I said.

"I am. My assistant Rae is in the powder room." His voice boomed deep like a softened kick-drum, emanating from a face that was just a cloud of black oily smoke. The smoke drifted across his body, a body that seemed unusually fit, in a $6,000 black-ivory Brookes-Stanton power suit, complete with a green and blue Black Watch tie. "Although if you meet her, please call her Doctor Stay rather than Rae. I abhor that people assume because I am a magical being that she is the least of our team."

I clawed myself to my feet and almost fell over again. Darkness did not move his legs when he walked, he just floated. He moved slowly to me and seemed to be gazing into my body. Then, he spoke. "Great men and women have your gift. They can leave their bodies and enter the bodies of animals. It works because they have immense discipline and iron wills that allow them to edit their mental selves with brutal and singular purpose, until the spark of their intellect and the tiniest of crumbs of their soul are all that is needed to travel to Virdea and enter the chosen mind. You, however, are not a great man."

As I stood, trying not to topple, he began to float around me. "I am sorry about my tendency for bluntness. You do bring interest to me. I am not aware of anyone else like you. You may not be great, but you are unique."

A coughing fit ran over me as I tried to clear my lungs of days of seizure. Darkness seemed not to notice. "Years ago, Rae taught me a modern game. It is called Dungeons and Dragons. Quite fun, you see. And really, a moral lesson if understood right, that no story can be told from the first person. Every story is, in fact, a tale of endless first persons linked; every quest is only completed when the hands of friends all grasp the flag at the top of the mountain and show the warriors in the valley below that only together do humans ascend."

His gestures were fluid, almost designed to put someone at ease. "I played the game for the first time, and I was a thief, and my party went in search of the unknown. By the end of the game, we had found it, but it took us all. Gates crashed down, and I unlocked them. Racist Orcs—and if I were an Akaoni, I would be upset about that—stumbled on us while plants screamed. I drank water from a pool that turned me pink. At the end, though, no points were awarded and no winning existed. We had all survived and profited in treasure, experience, and friendship."

I blinked at him. Was there a point, or was I just having an experience that would be edited out of the book? Perhaps to someday wind up in the extended director's cut of some unauthorized version of my novel. He gave a grumbling laugh and said, "My objective is, every other being in this story is learning something, or trying to, but you. You get sicker, and you discard friends, rather than ask them for help. Think on that, Lore-Master of Virdea."

There was a hiss from behind as Wandira Viking reacted to the title given me by Darkness. Darkness tipped his bowler and said, "The post is vacant, can you pay his first stipend?"

Wandira looked pinched. "Of course, Darkness."

"I must leave. We are doing Tomb of Horrors, and rumor is UrsulaK has rolled up a new wizard. Won't that be a treat?" He tipped his bowler; his hands were steaming oily smoke just like his face and left.

Wandira went to her desk and took out a leather lock case, opened it with a key from her fob, and said, "It's SIT$2,200 on appointment, and SIT$200 per month."

"What is a Tolar?" I asked.

She looked at me with a frown, "Slovenian currency, no longer valid in Slovenia. Slovenian is the seventh most common Earth language in Virdea, and the largest migration ever of humans to Virdea occurred in 1941CE where something like 300 Slovenian jews travelled from the top of a Slovenian Mountain to Virdea and ended up in Virdea around year 1500Z. Gold has always worked poorly as a currency for modern use, so when the Slovenians switched to the Euro, those of us that care about the economy of the second world ran the presses for a while in secret and printed a big batch of notes, enough for our tiny community. Impossible to counterfeit in a way magic cannot detect." She looked bemused for a second. "The Slovenians are the cleanest people in the world, but somehow the word for poor housekeeping came from their race name. The woman then put a wrapper of cash plus some loose bills into my hands. "Look, you are the new Lore-Master of Virdea, I hope you do something worthy of the title."

I put the money into my pocket. The small bills were creme colored with orange and pink writing and tinted images. "Fair enough, but what happened to the last Lore-Master, can I talk with him or her?"

"Sure, if you can find a part of her with a mouth. So far we just have a couple of ribs and a leg."

I walked out of the office into the bar. It seemed like this place had no off switch. There was a timeless feeling to the space. There was a double door leading to a hallway that said, "Doss." A set of stairs led to a landing with a sign that said, "Private Doss." What that meant was a mystery. Under the landing was a long bar that could have been ripped from the Gem around 1880. Thousands of bottles sat in front of a mirror, and there was a jar filled with Tolars that said, "Stump the Chump." A dozen bartenders served maybe 50 customers a constant stream of drinks, while a bar-back with gorilla arms brought out containers without stopping. Next to the bar was a series of stew pots, a pile of dripping bowls, and a mound of spoons. Next to that was bread piled high. The stew must be at least edible because plenty of patrons were partaking. Opposite the bar and the landing was a stage, dark right now. Three score tables stood in the open space before the stage, but space on the right was open, possibly for dancing.

Next to the main entrance, there was the corridor to the manager's office, and also a double door that said, "Services." Temporary signs were hung above that door that said, "Today: Weapon Exchange, Costumer, Magicker, Wellsman, Diviner, Epocher, Bank and Loan, Pawn, Companion." I was reading the sign when I felt a person by my side.

"You could use a companion."

After what Darkness had said, it was a strange synchronicity that shook me. "I beg your pardon?"

She was about 25, shorter than me, with long dusty hair held together by tight dreadlocks. She was at least partially Japanese, although her English showed she was likely born in the United States. She was dressed very oddly, in a green khirqah, sage hemp tie-pants, a large pin on her chest that said, "I heart Rumi," and a very real samurai sword. Crossed over her sailor's outfit was Russian leather ammunition pouches, onto one of which had been strapped a KCB-70 bayonet.

"I said you could use a companion. I can tell. I think I can. You aren't one of those professors writing a dissertation, are you?" She was forward, with a neutral face that was closed to the world.

I was confused, so I reached into my pocket for a bandana to wipe the sleep away from my face. In the bandana, though, was a silver object in a leather holder. I took it out and flipped it open. It was a badge with a crossed book and quill pen made of nickel and embossed in some gray and black metal. The woman in the warrior's outfit said, "Fuck, I am Akari. Given name Kuros."

"Anata ni oaidekiteureshīdesu, Kuros Akari."

She laughed. It was not the kitten laugh of a girl, but a mature understated haha of a laugh. "*Watashi wa manga o miru tame ni nihongo o benkyō shimashitaga, watashi wa eigo ga sukidesu."*

"Wakarimashita," I replied, although that was only half-true. When you learn Japanese by watching Shōgun, there is a limit to your conversation skills.

"Buy me a drink!" she said. Akari was no shy wall-flower. She had a way of walking like she deserved to be where she was; that confidence of space that reminded you of Summer Bishil walking by you on her way to get tea in Vancouver. She owns the street, and anyone else is there by her generous mood. It was not rudeness at all. Merely a solid understanding of her place in the order of the universe, and an unashamed understanding of her own value as a human. I could see Akari forcing her way past castle guards or perhaps attacking a small army of mercenaries.

We walked up to the bar and a man with a handlebar mustache and General Burns Mutton Chops asked, "What have you?"

Akari said, "Don Julio Real Tequila Anejo straight."

The bartender looked at her. "Akari, you have three Tolars left on your tab. How about a Glacier Bay?"

I smiled at the bartender and put 20 on the bar. "Why not get her the Don Julio?"

"She is a Companion you know. Contractable."

I asked, "Anything dishonorable or dangerous about that?"

He looked at Akari. "With her, nope, except she will strain your bar bills a bit if you take her on. Far as I know, she is not touched though. You maybe might want to talk to Gillia at the Companion Hall before you buy that drink."

Akari said, "Nick, don't queer things for me. I need this."

The bartender stepped back and returned with highball glass two fingers full of an amber liquid. She took the drink and swallowed a mouthful. "Standard contract, I follow you into danger, you make sure I get credit, especially let me have a boss mob once in a while. You know, someone at the end of the level. Pay my expenses and 50, plus one-fifth of the loot you acquire. And if you are a Paladin-type, give me a break on the rumpy-pumpy. I mean, share the wealth a little and throw me a bone or two when things are really exciting."

I nodded. "I agree. And as for rumpy-pumpy, whatever it is, I will throw you as many bones as I can once I find out how it works."

Akari and I ate pea soup, drank Budwine and Don Julio Tequila Anejo, and talked backstories. I ended up spending 50 on the carouse, but it was worth it. Akari took another 50 of mine and came back with some purchases. I had by then colonized a table; there was supposed to be live entertainment in the afternoon.

A pile of things landed on the table. Akari sat down with a smile. She pulled out a leather bag. "Bag of holding," she said. It was six inches deep and maybe had capacity for 500 milliliters. She took my walking stick and proceeded to shove it into the bag. The bag, without a bulge, swallowed it up. She then threw in my money, pack, and other odd items. The bag bulged a little at the end. "It's cheap, made in Thailand, but sturdy."

Next, she took a cardboard box out. It was labeled, "Hole, Portable, One (1)." Underneath in red letters, "NOT FOR LOOSE ITEMS, NOT FOR LIVING ITEMS, DO NOT CONSECT HOLES."

She opened the box and took a filmy, invisible thing from it. In her other hand, she took an instruction sheet. After reading it for a minute, she waved the hole in the air then shook it vigorously as she glanced at her watch. "Give me your arm."

I did so. She popped the bag in the hole, and then fixed the hole on my arm. "What is consect?" I asked.

"Placing a hole in a hole." She was deadpan in delivery, but I could tell she had a warm heart.

"What happens?" I asked.

"Nothing good," she replied.

The entertainment has started. Up first was a comedy act. Billed as Zuiko the Amazing, he wore a green cape and carried a skull with him. He introduced the skull as his uncle Teddy. "Take my skull, please!"

The comedian placed the skull on a chair and sang, "Me and My Shadow," occasionally saying, "take it Teddy," to silence.

I kept staring at the skull. It was William Mitchell, the Manes Zombie.

"You see that skull?" I asked Akari.

"Which one? The one inside the unfunny comedian's head, or the one on the chair?" She stood surveilling the room as if unsure a hoard of zombies might run in any second.

"The chair." I stared at the poor creature with pity.

"Yep. Not nice."

"More than you know. It is a thinking creature. A manes zombie." I had studied them to understand Mamma LeDeoux.

"I heard of those. Immortal. Where is its flesh?"

"The flesh wears away over the years."

"So, that poor thing knows it's on stage?"

"Basically.

"Shit." She looked at the stage with horror.

I took a page from my notebook and a space pen out and scribbled some things down. "Take this to the manager for me."

"Told you having a companion was a good idea." She took my note and went off.

The comedian was done and left the stage to a smattering applause when a guitar player took stage. It was an older man with an acoustic guitar. He set up a microphone by a chair, sat down, and started playing.

The room got quiet as the man played the tune. He did not use a pick; his rough fingers instead glided across the strings with long confidence. Around the room, the lights began to dim, and stars began to dance in the open sky. The bar mirror disappeared, and a giant soft pink moon began to rise. I felt, rather than saw, my table and chair come loose from the ground. Akari, floating in the darkness, came to rest in a chair by me. She reached over and grabbed my hand. "Virdea touched!"

I nodded. The stage was now an island and the tables of the guests, none of which made a sound as they strained to hear each note coming from the guitar, floating around it like a stage in the round. He suddenly changed speed and tone, breaking into a fast, almost bass version of the song "Sparks." His eyes were closed, and he played as if missing a note would cast him out into the depth of space, sending the audience crashing into a star. The faster he played; the more the guitar sounded like a locomotive crashing through walls of crystal mirrors. The tables started to dissolve, and soon those of us in the audience were just floating around an island that had been the stage. Just as the world was about to disappear, he changed songs again, this time an ancient Chacona. The stars began to flash vivid orange and red lights.

Then, it was over. I felt a flutter in my stomach as my chair dropped to the ground. Akari was on her chair screaming, and I knew my own quest centered on this man.

It was Randolph Homey, better known as Warsong.

PASSENGERS

DATE: JULY 1, 2018
LOCATION: 44.590278, -104.715278

Below six inches of soil was a door. It was made of scratch steel, sturdy and stainless, and coated on the edges by a black epoxy.

Two days before, Nelson McKeeby, dying author of little account; his companion, the fierce Akari; the protective spirit Grandfather bound into a magical hiking stick; a skull containing the soul of William Mitchell; the musical legend Randolph Homey; and a magical flamenco guitar, containing an ancient Shea Magicus spirit, sat down at a table with two bottles of overpriced tequila and several bowls of pea soup.

"You tried to contact me in Glendale," Homey said, drinking a shot of tequila.

I was sticking with Budwine. It was amazing to tastc the beverage of my childhood again. "I did. You are the missing link."

Randolph raised his hand, and a bartender brought him a beer to back the liquor. "Would you like a menu?" the server inquired.

I looked over at the stew pots, but the waiter stopped me. "We can handle more than bar fare."

The door was an old steel reinforced blast-proof. To its side was a control box that turned out to have a large lever in it. Lou Ball said, "Been going on 20 years no one pulled this. Not since the accident and the evacuation. You lot sure on this?" We had tracked Lou, the caretaker, down in a bar, but when we explained what he wanted, he had sobered up. At first, he had not wanted to help us break into the Dustin-Rhodes Reality labs, but when I offered him a thousand dollars, he shrugged. "Your funeral."

The only thing he had brought with him to break into his former place of employment was a heavy bag that said, "Enjoy St. Petersburg." Lou said, "We just dig away the dirt and pull the door hatch."

The digging had taken hours. The hatch was the work of seconds.

Randolph was staring at his empty plate. "You have to understand this from the beginning. I went to Virdea and learned music through magic, although people might say it was the opposite. For me, it was a place of pure creativity. I never wanted fame; I did not care for adulation. I just wanted to play. At first, I thought I was a prisoner, but then the Queen installed the Time Mirror, an object that lets you cross back and forth easily, if you have the magic inside of you, so I could leave when I wanted. And it turned out I did not want to go home."

A new act was on stage telling poetry. The speaker was a thin, bearded man who had a cautious, toothy grin and big glasses occupied the stage next to a sign that said, "Ryan Flavors, Poetry Reading, Fridays 11a and 2p." His reading had started rough in that the audience had been expecting "Flora Floozy and her Dance of the Gauze Merengue," but once Flattery was going the crowd quieted down. I turned my attention back to Warsong/Randolph.

Homey looked off into the distance of the great hall. "Virdea had always been a stepping stone of sorts for people with talents. It refines who you are. The Troubadour was a kid who read Karl Marx and liked being on stage. I wanted to noodle around on guitars. Each of us, though, were from families with different understandings. My parents were engineers; the Troubadour was supposed to be a great general. Only Virdea changed all that. It turned our building and fighting instincts to art."

Randolph turned to the audience enthralled by the complexities of the poet's words. "Then, it changed. I do not know how the Queen of Fire and Ice saw the change coming, but she started to talk about Earth being in trouble, and this the evil was fighting behind the lines. How can the warriors defend a society if the masters of ethics and the selfless wise are dying? How does the rule of law survive the death of the last law keeper?"

We descended into the darkness. Akari had her sword in one hand and the skull of a 19th-century pirate in another. Randolph held his guitar in front of him to allow its magical light to guide us into the dark. I used the Grandfather staff to steady my climb down. At the bottom, there was a large blast door. Lou Ball said, "Here is the key."

The key was a 24-volt lithium cell battery attached to a complex series of boxes, each with one or more probes coming off it.

He opened a side panel and began to slowly attach leads to it. When he attached the last, the cumbersome door slipped open quietly like its hinges were made of butter. Behind it was a blast-damaged room with pink glowing motes dancing around and a table upon which an envelope sat. We all walked into the room and stood watching the light show. Lou said, "On your own now." He turned and ran, the great door closing rapidly behind him.

Akari shrieked. "I think he has locked us in."

Randolph said, "It does not matter. I can feel it. They actually built a sustained transfer room."

I took the paper from the table. It was an advertisement for shuffleboard in Florida that said, "Virdea-yellow dit-dit-dash, Paris green dash-dash-dit-dash"

"So the Queen, along with a lot of other rulers, sends the Troubadour and I back to Earth. The idea was that our art would change the course of the gestalt and repair the upcoming crack in time. "

"Gestalt?" I asked.

"Our music, some other people from Virdea painting and writing and sculpting, and thousands upon thousands never Virdea touched at all. It adds up. You build a synergy, a gestalt. So when the crack came, we were there to hold the universe together for the year that it had to hold. And then, we were there to cure it afterward."

I drank some Budwine and looked at Homey. "I am sorry for being ignorant. The Crack?"

Randolph drank a sip from the water on the table. "The crack in time, 1968. Martin Luther King Jr. is killed April 4, 1968 by a French assassin, which was one of the first shots in a war designed to set off a world-wide destruction that would leave the Earth a wasteland. The Tlatelolco massacre, Ireland, Nixon. It was all coordinated. No one today wants to speak conspiracy because most evil starts with conspiracy theories, but it was the beginning of the end." The man was visibly nervous.

I felt fear in my stomach. "And your rock band the Portals stopped it?"

"We were part of it. Who knows how much we helped. It was close though. November 22nd was the day it turned. That day should be a holiday." It was like he was describing a funeral as a time of great hope, or a flood as a desired event that washed the road clear.

"Why?" I asked.

"The White Album and Plato's Stepchildren. Talk about a double whammy for good. Evil had been giving us a year of rope-a-dope, but that really knocked it back."

It was time for him to read my book. I took out the unfinished copy of *The Conspiracy of the Ravens* and slid it across the table. "Akari, can you get us all more to drink?"

An hour later, Randolph was looking a little pale when he put my book down. "I cannot say where I have read such utter garbage. And almost all of it seems true." He then turned to me. "The Troubadour did not conserve his magic. He was sure that the world was going to destroy itself, and soon. Why conserve something that he could use to save the world?"

"And he saved the world?"

"The world was saved, and the Troubadour was turned into a fame junkie and a pawn. It ate at him. Then, he decided one day to return to Virdea for rest, to let the magic rebuild. I told him to be really careful about that. I took him to the Rodehouse, and a lot of people said he was just too depleted to go back. Then, he tried."

"And what happened?"

"They said he was dead. He was buried quickly, no autopsy. But for weeks, people saw him around. People who knew him. I went to the Rodehouse and asked one of the people who knows about such things, but they said he was no longer alive."

That caught my attention. "They said he was dead?"

"No, just that he was no longer alive."

"See the spinning balls?" I asked. One of them is yellow and flashed with a dit-dit-dash sequence. Touch it, and we will be sucked to where we want in Virdea. The one that is green and goes dash-dash-dit-dash sends us to Paris."

Akari asked, "And the others?"

I shrugged. "Tear you into a million pieces, let's assume. Nothing good."

Randolph said, "Akari, you go to Virdea now, and keep the travelers from doing anything until we are there. Nelson and I need to go to Paris."

Akari jumped up and down. "Will this mean I get Virdea touched?"

I smiled and said, "I am not sure how you got into the Rodehouse, but you won't have trouble next time."

"I think he is not dead. How can he be in Virdea and not? I met people who were stuck inter-dimensionally. One of them warned me that my book could not be completely written if I did not save the Troubadour. And I think the way is with your help."

The news was hard on Randolph; I could tell. Dr. Rae Stay had joined us at my invitation and to explain what happened if you tried to get to Virdea and could not. She had a bit of fan shock over Randolph.

"So he is stuck, inter-dimensionally." Randolph asked Dr. Stay, wanting some confirmation.

"That is just it," Dr. Stay replied, "he can't be."

"Why not?" I asked.

"Darkness can always detect lost souls. He rescues them; it is like his cosmic job. Or he does not because he feels they need some time to consider their sins. Shoot, he may never pull Hitler's bacon out of the dimension cooker he is stuck in. Darkness does not forgive some things."

"Like genocide?" I asked.

Dr. Stay nodded "That and desecrating art. Oh, hurting cats is pretty bad; he really gets upset about that."

Randolph said, "So he would know where the Troubadour is."

"So would I. If he tried to break on through to Virdea, he might have faced a few weeks of hell, but we would have set him up in nil-space somewhere when we got to him. It's really complex, not just a wave of a wand. Anyway, either he never went back to Virdea, or someone else freed him. We had nothing to do with it."

An idea came to me. "So I, for example, could have freed him, space/time wise."

Dr. Stay laughed. "Oh, you have a promotion and now you think you are something Mr. McKeeby. Well, let me just caution you, it would take your power, plus another person with a name, and at least some other powerful foci to do it. And by do it, I mean shove his Soul to Virdea, 'cause his body is dead anyway once he fails to make it."

I saw Darkness walking in our direction. Or rather, his sinuous smokey glide. I turned quickly back to Rae. "Tell us one other thing—how do you push the Soul through? Why is it so difficult?"

Dr. Stay laughed again. "That is both easy and hard. All you need a Soul Scroll, but those things are tough to write. It is like a shopping list, only this list shows parts of a person's soul. Forget one thing, and horrible things happen. Shoot fire, we use the same scrolls to pull a soul instead of push, and I made one error with one comma, and they were cursed for life."

"How so?"

"He quit being a Steeler's fan and started worshipping the Tampa Bay Buccaneers. Talk about eternal damnation." She laughed, in high spirits, then drank more of her drink. "Anyway, no one will give you the Troubadour Rovane's scroll."

Darkness was now with us. He reached into his fancy suit and pulled out a scroll. In curlicue letters on a ribbon, it said, "Rovane."

WANDERING THE RIGHT BANK

DATE: JULY 3, 1971
LOCATION: THE MARSH, PARIS, FRANCE

17 Rue Beautreillis was a stone façade apartment in Paris. Randolph and I appeared in a little courtyard. We entered the building as a woman with a dog left, then I lead us to the third floor. Randolph tapped my shoulder as I walked into the hall.

"The Troubadour does not live here."

"Shit," I replied. "Fucking Wikipedia."

"No, the Internet is right, you are wrong. French buildings go "g-one-two-three." So this is the third floor."

I led us back to the stairs, and then corrected our mistake. Eovane's door was halfway down the hall, facing the street. The door was an easy mark, it only needed to be lifted to bend the lock, and no chain was on the inside. We got in.

"Angela?" Randolph said softly. I had forgotten that, unlike me, he was an intimate friend of the Troubadour's and had known Angela Shield in his youth. I checked the apartment quickly and came back, "No one here."

Randolph nodded to the bathroom. I went to it and opened the door.

To someone not Virdea touched, it would not have looked like anything in particular. The Troubadour sat in cold bath water, waxy, and dead. To a Virdea touched, though, it was obvious. He had been trying to get to Virdea. What theory of travel he was using or if it would have worked is up in the air. He had gotten part of the way there and was now stuck.

Randolph had his guitar on his back. He brought it around and began playing, just jamming progressions of chords, really letting his heart lead his playing. At the same time, I took a package of matches from my pocket, lit the scroll, and threw it at the lights.

There was a second when time stopped. I could feel this intense negative pressure that popped my psychic ears and made my brain feel like it was swelling. Then it ended. Randolph and I were standing alone in a cold room, looking at a fallen friend.

Randolph did not speak as we boarded a transatlantic flight to New York from Paris. It was odd to find tickets, passports, and money waiting for us at the counter, but there it was. By now, I knew how it happened, so the weirdness was more a measure over the slickness that the universe ran, rather than any desire to argue with fate. When we landed in New York I threw my passport away, and we both took a train back to Wyoming. We went out to the laboratory expecting to have to steal one of those complex door openers, but we found the doors were open, and a long-haired, blue jean wearing man with a white cotton shirt was sitting among the pulsing globes of color. Next to him was a stack of tourist brochures, one of which was for a shuffleboard tournament being held in next century. I borrowed it, somc paper, and wrote up the notes we had found. I then wrote another letter and said, "Do you mind sending this to Western Union?" I gave him the rest of my money, and Randolph and I made the final transition to Virdea.

AN IMPOSSIBLE BOSS

DATE: FEBRUARY 3, 2018
LOCATION: PETERBOROUGH, NEW HAMPSHIRE

Rochelle Standish had spent most of her life in school. She had studied and mastered academic subjects and wrote papers and done everything every professor had ever told her to do. She had then graduated, only to discover that all of those degrees meant exactly dick. No one would hire her for anything more than 10 bucks an hour as a barista.

The pay working for Mr. McKeeby was better, but the frustration was higher. He was always having her do crazy things such do research that was absolutely insane and deal with oddball people. And it was getting worse. Bail him out of jail, send his duplicate license, book a bus to here, have his stuff picked up from a campsite and delivered there.

And endless freak show requests for research. New Orleans voodoo, children's literature, a picture of Janis Joplin. She dreamed one day of a nature non-profit rescuing her from this hell.

Then the letter came through. It was a drop-mail from Western Union, delayed until the day before. In the Western Union envelope was a hand-written letter that said,

Rochelle,

Please put Akari Omi on the payroll as a companion. Documents to follow.

Order two bottles of Don Julio Real Tequila Anejo. Put it in with the rest of the booze.

Send a letter c/o the management to the Rodehouse and ask if they would, against my account, have passports and money waiting for Mr. Homey and I on July 4th, 1971 at the Paris United desk.

Nelson

"For fuck's sake," she said when reading the memo.

THE COURT OF THE BIPOLAR QUEEN

DATE: 22ND DAY OF THE RAM, 3684
LOCATION: THE EMERALD CITY, VIRDEA

Kelle had spent two days preparing for the meeting with the Queen. The city itself was in turmoil from a stomach ailment with fear borne of any premodern society that such an ailment would turn to a terrible, murderous beast, tearing up the people of the town in its invisible fangs. Despite this, Kelle was able to have a dress made for her, and she made sure Rains-a-Lot and Ivy were properly outfitted for the most important meeting of their lives.

For most of the endless trek from the Meadows, the Troubadour had been proudly claiming that the Queen of Fire and Ice could solve their problems. She was the most powerful monarch in the lands of Virdea, and more than just powerful, she was also one of the Nine Wizards. Her beauty was said to be incomparable, though she had never married.

Now, though, the Troubadour had been missing for many days, and she had to make their appointment for the Queen's levee without him. The theory was that any citizen or visitor to the lands of the Queen could approach her and ask for boon, counsel, or aid. In reality, everyone else was asking for such things, and there was a certain stickiness in the situation. Despite this, she had almost been rushed into her appointment even if the courtiers she spoke to claimed it was unlikely the Queen would help.

And the fact was their backs were to a wall. There was only so much farther they could flee as the powers of three great enemies closed in on them. Two of their enemies wanted to execute the four of them publicly, while the third would use her companions as pawns to assure her own obedience.

Besides, they were tired. Despite magical healing, Ivy was distant and limped on his wounds. She felt he had made some breakthrough, but really needed time to process it. Rains-a-Lot had grown sterner and even more silent as day after day of vigilance took its toll.

She never forgot they worked for a faceless corporation. When she had first contacted the FBI, her goal had been to find a research lab that she could create a portable dimension gate machine in, which would allow her to put some real space between her and Judius. She wondered who Ivy and Rains-a-Lot would follow if their company got back in contact with her. They had all been living for the day that the great Queen would be before them, with no thought of where to go after.

Then there were the ravens. Dozens of times, they had interceded to the travelers' benefits, waving them away from danger and directing them to aid. Yet, in all that time, no one could say why.

She was lost in reverie standing next to Mamma LeDeoux, who quietly rumbled in idle, when Ivy and Rains-a-Lot came to sudden motion. A young woman dressed in a cute sailor's suit and carrying a samurai sword was walking toward her with purpose. The woman was just meters away when she found herself staring at Ivy's French battle rifle and Rains-a-Lot's ancient Smith and Wesson pistol.

She must have been fearless because she stared right at Kelle and said, "I am Akari, family name Omi, Companion to the Lore-Master of Virdea. I am to ask a boon of you, Dr. Brainerd.

Kelle was impressed. She should get one of these companions to send messages for her. "Go ahead Sailor Moon, tell the barrel riders about this boon."

"My Companion Lore-Master and the former Court Musician, Warsong would request you delay your entry to see the Queen until it can be arranged for you to accompany the Troubadour, who's elected to follow a quest with you."

"I am not sure how long I can delay."

Kelle saw Jaze Jakobian, dressed in red and blue court finery, approaching. She waved him over. The man was an officious prig and number-counter, but he was not a bad sort.

"Dr. Brainerd," he said, bowing.

"Master Jakobian. Is there much time before we are scheduled?"

"I assure you, any minute now."

"That is just it. I need a minute. Two of my retinue are not yet here."

Jakobian frowned. "That is irregular; they are not vetted."

"I believe they are. They are known as Warsong and the Troubadour."

"Doctor, I can assure you if you can produce those two, a delay of even an hour would be overlooked."

"They can be produced!" The yell came from the Troubadour who was followed by an older man with a raven on his shoulder.

Jakobian let out a high squeal. "Master Warsong."

Warsong stepped forward and hugged the court minder, the first person in all of history who had ever made the attempt. Jakobian excused himself and ran to the crier, Ottobelia who yelled, "The Travelers and the Conspiracy of the Ravens."

"As we practiced!" Kelle yelled as music came up with thumping rhythm on Mamma's speakers. The song "No New Tale to Tell" played.

Ivy and Rains-a-Lot stepped off first. Marching heel-to-toe at the beat of the song and swinging their bodies left and right, they carried their rifles at presentation. Kelle had gotten them loose green cavaliers' rigs. Looking like she had rehearsed with them, Akari held forward her own sword and stepped off after them. When Rains-a-Lot and Ivy began doing the fancy manual, she began to whirl her sword in time, and when the rifles went into the air, the sword went with them in a flashing spin.

Kelle was about to step off herself when Warsong and the Troubadour pushed forward. Unlike the disciplined March, both of them took up a ribald counter-step to the music that was purposely out of sync. Then, the conspiracy flew in, each one holding some piece of cloth, each one a different color. The audience cheered as Kelle stepped off with the Chevy, and it appeared that the ravens dropped the cloth bits to cover the floor in front of Kelle.

At the balk point, Ivy and Rains-a-Lot fell into a countermarch, arriving echelon left, while Warsong and the Troubadour swept right. Kelle arrived at the middle of the balk point and genuflected with a wide curtsy, then said, "Queen!"

The music stopped and the Queen said, "I see before me Warsong and the Troubadour in your retinue. Do they represent you?"

"They are friends on a long journey, High Queen," Kelle could see a slightly deflated Sackbutt player in Lederhosen next to the Queen. He was not smiling at all.

"You have a favor to ask? I say this to be official, although I know of and understand your quest."

Kelle put every mote of magic she could into each syllable of her next sentence. "We ask the boons of protection, advice, and succor."

The Queen's angular face looked down at the Troubadour and Warsong. "I had planned to send you off. You called this down on yourself when you killed a monarch. This is not to say I do not understand it, at least in some ways.

"But then you enter my court with a currency I did not know you possess. The court owes Warsong and the Troubadour in the coin of honor. A coin we wish we had in our purse in sufficient quantity to bestow on them. A compromise thus is called for. Mistress of State!"

An elaborately gowned man stepped forward. "Your Majesty."

She looked at the crowd then said, "What is the international status?"

"We have numerous filings. Devitu d' Cavallu claimant of the Yellow Throne claims rights to the Travelers based upon the theory of Forte Maine..."

A man in a fox-fur outfit stepped out of the crowd of the court and said, "My Queen, I am Hasso and represent the true Yellow King. You must realize your majesty entertains mass murderers who, our research has revealed, run a brothel for underage children in Maysport, who have been linked with cases of wanton destruction across the continent, and who hold insult contests against the Queen at every opportunity."

There was silence. The Queen turned to Hasso and said, "My dear visitor from Gulled Republica, sir. You have interrupted a court minister. You have also forgotten your place. The role of the so-called Foxes of News is to keep the unintelligent chasing shadows and to break apart strong nations from inside with unprovable gossip. If you step forward again unasked, I WILL HAVE YOUR FUCKING HEAD!" Calming slightly, the Queen said, "Continue, Minister."

"My Queen. Lord Devitu d' Cavallu and Lord Shibbula each offer strong arguments based upon the death of the Yellow King. A third army under the Wizard of the Obsidian Tower claims escaped spousal rights, which we reject." She stepped back into place among the courtiers.

The Queen said, "Any of my other courtiers wish to speak?"

Admiral Gane stepped forward. "The combined forces of the three armies gathering against us is 6,000 souls. They have heroes, magic, and initiative on us. There is little chance the army could face even one opponent now with the flux upon us. If any of those two find common cause, it will not be an issue of us giving up the travelers, it will be a question of keeping the city from falling."

The Queen turned back to the crowd for a second. Dress makers were always commenting on her fashion sense, and artists forever sketching what she wore, but Kelle had heard a rumor and saw that it was true. Her dress was a cunning composite. Instead of a single length of cloth, her dress was made by combining an emerald greed brocaded vest, a red and green veneer jacket, and a floor-length skirt of brushed worsted. Far from being a dresser's nightmare, the ensemble could be assembled quite handily by the Queen herself, and a dressing maid would be a convenience rather than a requirement. There was no crinoline cage, no stress hooks, and no canvas frame holding the contraption together in defiance of gravity. Mary, Queen of Scots wore a dress even on the most common of occasions into which she could secrete dog treats, eating utensils, water, alms, a small bible, and even her pet dog. In the case of the Queen of Fire and Ice, under the dress, you only had a Queen.

When she turned around, her hard face showed compassion. "Dr. Brainerd, please step forward."

Kelle felt her stomach jerk. She thought she was immune to royalty worship, but suddenly, she understood the allure. She preferred democracy despite years of reading everyone from the Daily Worker to the National Rifle Association bash democracy while pretending to laud it. Still, here was a woman who had power, knew its limits but also its possibilities, and knew how to decide. It was strong stuff. She solemnly stepped forward.

"Dr. Brainerd, I am sorry to be the goal of your quest and to end it differently than you desired. To you, this may seem like I am a puppet master who hides behind a curtain pulling strings, but I assure you, I cannot give you what you wish. Still, you arrive bearing a powerful argument in the form of two people for whom my court is always open, Masters Warsong and Troubadour.

"To the three powers that request Dr. Brainerd and her people as their own, if one of you, without significant opposition of the other two, shall encamp at the ruins of Tell Vabis at Sweetwater Oasis, for a period of three days, on day four, I will hand over the Travelers."

Kelle and her friends were escorted to the door. On the way out, Kelle leaned into Ivy who broke his disciplined march to touch her on the shoulder. The touch told her everything she would need to know about his love.

MEGGIDO

DATE: 16TH DAY OF THE RABBIT, 3684
LOCATION: EMERALD CITY, VIRDEA

It is said by some great minds, namely, Dr. Kelle Brainerd, that the greatest city of Virdea exists to confound the visitors from Earth. The reasoning behind this is that the city is, in every way, a study of dualism. The city is said to be walled, but the wall is not one that stands fourth, tall and proud, like a curtain around the city. The wall instead retains a mound of soil that has grown over the years and upon which the city is built, like a terrace in a farmer's garden.

Another odd fact, the city is said to be the greatest human community in Virdea, but humans are distinctly in the minority. Haguni, the Fey, Akaoni, GoKabi, Treeheards and Qurabaca all roam the cities, serving the city nearly interchangeably as merchants, soldiers, administrators, artists, scholars, and artisans. The effect is that there is no Emerald City food style, or art movement, or anything of the sort. If you search for it, a guide will say, you can find it. Or worse, it will find you.

The city is described hundreds of times in the literature of Virdea, but those descriptions are, at best, generational. Many of the buildings are formed from the great Southern banyan and are constantly growing and changing, while a distinct number of other buildings are created by gray mud bricks which last not more than a decade of monsoons before they collapse and are replaced by new mud brick buildings. It is even futile to discuss issues of dimension for the city. City engineers note that the city is growing upward, but that the shifting river occasionally causes parts to sag or even collapse. Where the river is too good at undermining the city, banyans came to the rescue, but even the banyans are of a mind of their own about this and sometimes signal a migration, giving way to the water. Mud banks upstream grow heavy with silt and are soon mined for bricks, while ancient bricks exposed to the flow of water erode and see their being migrate down to become the gray-white beaches of the Southern shores.

The residents of the Green City refer to where they live as a quadrant. This leads a visitor from Earth to assume it is divided into four portions. In fact, there are eight named quadrants: Boardwalk, The Docks, Old Gaslight, The Haguni Quarter, The University, Tradeside, Testaments, and Mudside, which itself can confuse people because the laws of the city-state definitively that the city proper "is the space existing inside the physical walls of the community," and Mudside is not even on the same island. You would have to know the precedent that "Awater barrier capable of carrying an ocean-going ship shall be considered a wall." Thus, Boardwalk and Mudside are not outside of the city, but they are vibrant and ever-changing parts of the city itself.

The dualism of the city extends to its environs, the so-called curtilage of Emerald City. The Queen of Fire and Ice rules over a constellation of 11 smaller city-states, but legally this is a voluntary trade union designed to balance the power in the Delta region with other trade powers. When a scholar looks at the land under direct control of the Queen, it consists of just 80,000 hectares of land divided evenly between the plains of Meggido and the wetlands formed by the Rejava, the greatest river in Virdea. The wetlands portion of it, just shy of 35,000 hectares, is impassable to armies that would bog into the deep mud, but it also represents an unpleasant prospect in that the land is extensively farmed by the Haguni who basically feed the city along with their great fishing fleet. Think aquatic velociraptors (Jurassic Park, not horrible chicken) and you can understand why no army wants to march through this land to the gates of the great city. The rumor that the Haguni can mulch anything is absolutely true.

On the other side is Meggido, a clay substrate plain that measures 200 kilometers by 220 kilometers in size. Surprisingly, considering how much water falls from the sky in the region and how much flows through the delta, Meggido has only six substantial sources of water, all ground water springs. Otherwise, the best that can be said of this swath of land is that the sheer variety of flowering plants is stunning.

Thus, a visitor to the city passes either through hot, dragon filled swamps or across a surprisingly arid and long expanse of rust-colored prairie before they reach the city. It is no wonder that even the name of the city seems to be in flux. Is it the Green City, the Emerald City, the Queen's City, or the Great City? Use any of these names and no one will complain, except scholars who are generally kept in barrels and brought out on All Fool's Day to prognosticate on the end of winter before being returned to their oaken homes.

Knowing what we know about the Emerald City, we can turn our attention to the great plain of Meggido. It represents the strategic challenge that must be met before the city can be invested by an invading army and is a feature of many scrolls on tactics written in Virdea. First, the issue of water and supplies looms large. Unless your army is mechanical, or perhaps if it can eat silvergrass and alumroot, taking Meggido is a process of controlling a given set of the groundwater sources available. An army of 10,000, which is pretty good for Virdea, can cover at most a rectangle two kilometers across, considering the reach of a warrior's glaive. So the process every army likely will follow is to capture water sources while outflanking the Emerald City-based defenders who rarely amount too much in numbers but are often highly skilled.

Despite endless ink applied to endless scrolls in the theoretical discussion of the investment of the Emerald City by a foreign force, before 3684, it had never been tried. The fact was that most of the people who might try it had easier targets closer at hand. In reading the history of Europe, one should not wonder why France or Germany clash so often, but instead, they should wonder why Belgium is usually the first to get its ass kicked in any war in Europe. The little country, divided in language and sometimes religion, had no natural defensive barriers, but if you really understand how things work, it had a kickass cheese industry thousands of years old. So the question moves from why invade Belgium to why bother invading France or Germany?

You can see why the Romans, facing the Rhine, and a bunch of barbarians who put butter in their hair, said fuck it and took on the Belgae. It is a lot easier, and you can have fondue afterward.

The gentle reader will have to forgive me if I shy away from describing the 27-day Meggido campaign. From the first clash of Shibbula and Devitu d' Cavallu's soldiers on the 18th day of the month of the Rabbit, z3684, to the final debacle, it was obvious to all involved that the three parties were fighting for more than the right to capture four Travelers, but they had set their sight on taking over the Emerald City. It was a case of a prize that was too valuable and seemed too easy to pluck, being conveniently located next to a prize you wanted anyway.

There are several classic works published on the campaign that a reader who wants a day-by-day discussion of the battle can refer to. Foe's classical *Dawn with Twenty-Score Rogues* is a detailed account of Shibbula's fast-moving campaign aimed at destroying the supply lines of his two antagonists. Hilby Foote's often ignored *They Marched Like Men*, tries to cover the maneuvers of all three armies, and provides an excellent insight into Devitu d' Cavallu's efforts to fortify the main oasis points as the Wizard of the Obsidian Tower tried to keep his forces unified, seeking a decisive battle. And of course, the anti-war saga written by an anonymous monk many years later, "*Bleeding Yellow in a Plain of Red*," with its evocative scenes of the rations soldiers carried and their struggles with lack of water and terrible wind storms really brings home the human costs of the struggle.

The main issue that a fourth person can have with any of this is that they are all beside the point. Battles were fought, men struggled and died, leaders filled with hubris made speeches tender and mistaken, and none of it mattered at all. In the end, none of the great armies won, there was only one charge and one melee that mattered, and the city-state survived only because her enemies failed to consider that in Virdea "Karma is a bitch."

Move your sight back to the 16th day of the Rabbit and consider Kelle Brainerd. If, someday, someone designs a board game about the Meggido campaign, she will be a small die-cut, cardboard piece, colored blue, with no attack number, a one defense, and a +70 effects rating, highest in the game. That is because as soon as the campaign started, Dr. Brainerd set up in a spare room of the palace with a map, hundreds of wooden figures representing men and resources, a huge stack of blank paper, and the willing labor of around 50 people and over 900 ravens.

Now, only a very silly person, or a person who knows the deepest truths about ravens, would ever create a story where these birds fly messages about. Ravens are proud and intelligent, and they are motivated by trust and friendship. Ravens that have voluntarily joined a conspiracy, though, will do many un-raven like things. It is one of the signs that a conspiracy exists. They will also do a lot of raven like things for un-raven-like reasons.

With three armies locked in combat across a huge expanse of clay barrens, infiltrating any but the best commandos into their midst was suicide. Instead, Kelle began to send out small flights of loyal birds.

Some of those flights stole things and returned them to Kelle. Thousands of coins, pieces of jewelry, steel pins that held armor together, stopcocks for water containers... she had a list and ravens stole as many as they could. They also dropped half-finished letters purported from one commander to another talking about how taking money from the pockets of the men was helping finance the campaign.

As the armies moved away from their bases of supply, the ravens then started to inflict minor sabotage. Kelle, aware of the terrible stomach virus raging in the city, used spoiled eggs to nurture that virus, dried the egg matter, put it into tea sachets, and had the sachets dropped into water containers and even springs. The fast running springs could not be fouled for long, but by the time they ran clean hundreds of soldiers were sick. Water containers were even more vulnerable as they might be refilled hundreds of times before their contamination was detected.

The curious thing about these tactics was that armies in Virdea knew about the magical ways that they could be compromised about the smallest creatures and took steps to prevent it. The problem was that none of the three armies were professional in the sense that they were seasoned campaigners with discipline and knowledge of the craft of war. For reasons of their own, each of the leaders of the competing armies had relied on rapidly raising the scum of the earth by raiding prisons, incorporating bands of scorchers, gathering up deserters, and throwing weapons into the hands of peasants to form their armies. The professional armies of the Yellow King were captives in the meadows, moldering in shallow graves in a dozen battle sites since the civil war struck that nation, or had fled. The Wizard of the Obsidian Tower had never had an army, just mercenaries, and would never trust the serfs of his plantations with weapons.

It was so easy to poison the water and the will of the armies that the ravens grew cocky. Voles, normally a food source, were now part of a sick raven game. A fight of ravens would scoop up two score voles and dive bomb them into stacks of grain, where the voles would have a delirious feast for two days, wondering what heaven their traditional enemies had given them. Then, the ravens would return and feast on the fattened voles who then discovered that sometimes a feast is too good to be true.

The effect of this was a slow withering of the armies as they fought each other and struggled to reach the gates of the Emerald City. None of them, it turned out, turned north as the Queen had instructed them to if they wanted her to voluntarily give over the travelers.

While the three armies withered, Kelle went about putting together her own small army. On the 19th, five members of the Art Commune, each warriors of renown in Virdea, were transported from the top of Mount Washington to the Emerald City and announced their choice to support the travelers. On the 20th, seven soldiers from the deep delta came, having heard that history was to be made in an uneven fight.

There is a legend during the Middle Ages that two armies were facing each other in what could have been a bloody battle across a narrow bridge, when the leaders of the two sides decided to talk it over. It was decided that each side would have 50 warriors in their team, and the winning team would be victor, while the losing team would retire from the field.

The little battle was delayed and delayed again as knights sent messengers from across the region that they desired to fight in the battle of the hundred. The reason the crossing was being contested was lost, and soon it was just a case of standing up to the awful British or terrible French or maybe against everyone standing on the left side of a river. The roster was changed as more prestigious knights arrived, until it was the all-stars game of the first decade of the 14th century. The battle was fought, many died, but forever after, people who had been one of the hundred had one over someone who had not.

Maybe that was going on here, but I like to think that Kelle's cause was resonating with people, and those people had decided that it was time for them to step up and be heard. In a week, 50 warriors and magic users were present in Kelle's camp. There was Regulus of the Sword, Warhammer, the Wizard of the Firth, and Torch, the fire chantress. Others quietly joined. Delbert Devine and Deanna Fortress, waiting on the appearance of the CEO of Brain Trust, felt they had nothing better to do, so they joined the army as well. Delbert was surprised when Rains-a-Lot and Ivy saw him standing with the other warriors, a French Mle 1949/56 rifle slung on his shoulders, yet they said nothing. They just nodded as if they expected nothing else.

Near the Emerald City, two armies became one. There has aways been a curtain of rumor around this, but what appears to have happened was that Devitu d' Cavallu was berating his news fox Hassu, when the man suddenly snapped. In terms of fighting power, he was hardly in the same class of Devitu d' Cavallu, but for one minute, he was a fierce burst of light. He stabbed the pretender to the Yellow throne repeatedly and then talked the followers of the slain pretender over to the side of Shibbula.

Shibbula had hardly been in charge of the combined host of the Yellow King for a day when he suddenly decided to merge his army with that of the Wizard of the Obsidian Tower. I wish, as an omnipotent neutral observer, I could tell you why he did this. There are lots of logical reasons for it, from having a depleted force to concern that the Emerald City might make a deal with the Wizard. I just know the force that approached the defensive positions of the Travelers was united and under joint command.

The city had been preparing with its weakened forces to defend gates against the invaders, but the people were shocked on the morning of the 22nd to awake to find a small band of around 100 people, armored and armed for battle, marching from the central square to the Lattice Gate. A handful of musicians played as they walked, while a small drum corps had turned out in support.

The people of the Emerald City left their houses and watched in awe. Here were 100 walking to face 2,000 or more, walking to their deaths, or worse.

It is here that as the fourth person I must leave you mid-chapter. It is best you see the coming battle from the eyes of an actual veteran. To tell the truth, I ducked out early at Little Big Horn; also, it's easier on the conscience.

Ivy had spent so many years in the military that marching was nothing. You marched in your sleep, usually, the lizard part of your brain pushing your feet forward and back.

Now, though, it was like the march at the end of the war when he was young. Wearing a helmet too big for his head, a uniform he did not realize he merited, and a rank he had only discovered was his a week before, he had been shoved into the ranks of the 13th Demi-Brigade, handed a Garand that he did not even know how to load topped with a bayonet, and told not to step on the man in front of him.

Then, he had seen everything like a filmstrip rolling past him. Cheering crowds of people who he had never seen smile before. Bands playing La Marseillaise, and Yankee Doodle set to the quick step. Spahis coming to attention guarding the route, their silver helmets as foreign as their great horses. And explosion of relief that the war was over, no one truly understanding that hell still existed just a few years in the future.

Marching through the city, Ivy felt this sense of honor and doom flowing like sugary syrup off the walls of the gray brick or greed living buildings. Would the armies turn back once they had destroyed the last stand of the travelers? Or would they still take the disease-riddled city, supine before them? And should they honor the Travelers, or hate them?

What puzzled Ivy the most was the dozens of people marching with them who could not possibly think they had a place in this fight. The Yellow King and the Wizard of the Obsidian Tower were both hated, but hate does not, in Ivy's understanding of the world, make a reason to leave a comfortable life to die for a forlorn hope to protect people who you could not possibly know.

Despite this, Ivy was content. For his entire life, he had sought a home, thinking that someplace would be where he could finally rest. He had fought in Indochina out of memories of a childhood in the streets of Saigon, noodle stalls, and the kiss of love in darkened, rainy streets. And that street proved to be without joy, a false front that ate his youth and tore his dreams from him.

Now though, he knew. Home was Dr. Kelle Brainerd. Home was Rains-a-Lot. Home was a purple 1957 Chevy with the soul of a 19th century macumba in it. Home was where his loved ones were. They had each taught him this.

They marched into the sunshine out of the city gate. He had crawled this same path on nights before, lugging bags of what the city vendors called dew dripping, rolling barrels of fish oil, and carefully carrying little boxes of Prometheus cakes. Now, he walked across the bridge upright with the sun in on his back.

He smiled to himself as he syncopated his marching step. It was a wives tale, a superstitious piece of nonsense, but old soldiers thought if a marching army crossed a bridge in step, the bridge would collapse. In reality, it was a joke that allowed the old timers to play games.

He was at the lead of 30 named warriors of Virdea, so he thought a cadence song was in order. "Cadence call, Commence!" Ivy started to sign R.E. M's "Losing

My Religion," and as he would sign one line, the response was others signing the next one or two.

A guitar caught the call and response, as did a few drummers, and soon the entire column was singing the cadence.

It was called Salta Ghol. It was a salt lick that the city used to flood to produce brine. Now, it was a desolate 20 hectares of low pan with a central mound. For the past several days, they had been using sandbags to turn the mound into a hedgehog. The group came to a stop, flights of ravens spinning above them. A snowy white owl and a raven came to rest on Mamma LeDeoux, and the raven dances a little tattoo.

The warrior named Akari said, "The three armies are one, and they have our scent."

Ivy said, 'Spies, no doubt."

Kelle looked at him with a smile. "This is it."

Ivy said, "It seems so, what do you think Rains-a-Lot?"

"Getting surrounded is a great strategy," Rains-a-Lot replied acidly.

There was a commotion. Ivy saw Rains-a-Lot straighten up, but they had known this was coming. Delbert Devine had been, months and dimensions ago, their boss. They were pretty much resigned from Dustin-Rhodes, but they still respected their boss. And their boss was now leading 10 dark-suited bruisers into the salt pan, along with a single short man who looked like a beat poet.

Kelle lost her smile. "Dad!"

"Kelle, dear," he replied, walking up to them. "Thank you, Delbert," he said to the man who walked with him.

"Don't you call me a cloven hoofed animal," she said angrily.

Ivy had his rifle off his shoulder as did Rains-a-Lot, and he started advancing on the heavies. The heavies had toy rifles, flat black plastic with curved magazines. Their rifles came up with amazing precision.

Kelle's father said, "Daughter, I did not come here for a firefight."

"Then what the fuck did you come here for?" she questioned angrily.

"We should talk alone," he said calmly, looking at Ivy and Rains-a-Lot.

"Daddy, I am about to have a last stand in an alternate universe. Can't we do this later, or better yet, never?" Kelle stamped her foot, looking about 10 years old in front of her father.

Ivy noted Kelle's father was wearing a turtleneck. It did not look comfortable, but what could Ivy tell? His black hair and goatee were also annoying.

"Daughter, I have pancreas cancer. Stage IV. Very soon you will be the Chief Officer of Brain Trust. I need to talk to you about it," he continued.

Kelle replied, "Dad, go back to New Jersey. If I live through this battle, then I promise to spend a month with you before you kick off. If this turns out dry, then what does it matter?"

"I understand. New Jersey, soon as you can." He nodded at his men, and they turned to leave. He turned to Delbert and said, "Are you coming?"

"Sir, Ms. Fortress and I can stay to see Dr. Brainerd to you after the battle," Delbert replied.

"Good." He walked off through the salt pan, flanked by 20 men in suits.

Akari said, "He did not offer to help with the battle?"

Kelle said, "He is not that sort of father."

Ivy smiled at the stronghold of the travelers. Kelle had designed it, and although she claimed to have never seen the movie, it looked just like a Beau Gest set. The hard salt pan, white and forbidding, could be a desert while the line of trees less than a kilometer way marked the edge of the fecund river.

Ivy had a very special mission. He chose a loop at the right of the fort where he could see both a berm several hundred meters behind the fortress, which held back the river from swamping the salt pan, and the main track that armored men could take in attacking the fortification. A few of the travelers had rifles, most French army weapons originally from Dustin-Rhodes stocks, but most of the firepower in the fort was traditional Virdea muscle powered missile weapons and magic.

The fort was sitting on a slant well which provided endless water and had dugouts and overhead protection. A ton of food was good for feeding the group for two weeks. They had 10 tons.

It was the afternoon when a horseman appeared on the rim of the salt pan. He checked his horse, spun, and rode away.

Half an hour later, another horse appeared. He rode to the ersatz fortress and stopped in front of the gate. "I am to talk to Kelle Brainerd!"

Kelle came to the citadel wall and said, "Talk!"

"My lord Wizard is interested in your safety. Come forth, and you will be protected from the wrath of the Yellow King. There need only be three crucifixes here today," the horseman said.

"Let me think about it," she replied.

Ivy stuck his head up. His MAS 1949/56 had a great scope, an issue APX. He was about 200 meters from the horseman who was holding a fluttering flag.

Kelle stuck her head back up. "He needs to get me a case of Budwine soda, a copy of the board game Clue, and a six-inch long pink dildo."

"I am sure we can work that out when you are free from that rabble," the horseman answered.

"What about the crucifix posts for my friends, did you get the scratchy types or the smooth comfortable types?" she asked.

The horseman grimaced, "I am sorry; I do not know what you mean."

"Then get the fuck out and send someone who can negotiate," she yelled.

With that, Ivy fired. It was a tough shot, but he shattered the wooden pole with the white flag he carried and caused it to fall from the horseman's hands. The horseman charged away.

Ten minutes later, a thousand soldiers charged over the end of the pan and toward the fortress. Ivy saw a cloud of ravens take to the sky and the hundred defenders rise, bows, rifles, and slings at ready.

His job was different. He turned back to the berm. He had marched off this shot and set up wind flags the night before. Ivy took a deep breath, then started his relaxation routine. He centered the scope on a tiny red piece of cloth. The cloth was attached to a box of Prometheus bricks, stacked on bags of salt peter, tamped by sandbags. He let out his breath, squeezed the trigger, and fired.

A second later, the berm disappeared in a blast, followed by a wall of water. He turned and looked at the charging army. It stopped in its tracks, and some started to back away. The water was a wall of force, and the people tiny dots in the pan. The water moved fast, reaching the soldiers in a minute, and rising to their knees in two.

Then, it stopped rising. The pan was soaking in water like a sponge, no matter how much the river dumped in; the pan soaked it up. Ivy could see the Wizard standing next to the so-called Yellow King. He yelled, "Water, Kelle? Do you think you can kill the greatest Wizard in all of Virdea with a splash of water?"

Kelle had moved to sit on the parapet, dangling her feet between the crenelation. It struck Ivy he loved Kelle in a way he thought was dead. Here she was victorious, and her ignorant enemy, a person who had chased her for years, who even now crowed his superiority, made her sad.

It was the first group, only 20 meters from the mound of soil on which the castle stood that started to cry out first. The soil was sucking in water, but the water mixing with the soil was making a terrible mud. When the salt had left the pan, what was left was a viscous clay heavy mud. It had been Kelle, scouting for where to fight, who had seen the bones of Meggido deer.

The Wizard, in the middle of his men, found that his own feet were stuck, and that the water continued to rise. Travelers and their allies started to line the battlements of the hodgepodge fort, watching the water climb slowly.

Judius cast spells and the water boiled. He tried apparition, but it failed. No spirit came to his aid, and no cantrip gave him succor. Soon, he slipped below the water.

Once it was safe, Kelle said, “Launch the rafts, save who you can.” Ivy watched as she turned and cried.

INVESTING A NEW QUEEN

DATE: 9TH DAY OF THE BEAR, 3685
LOCATION: THE CITY OF GLASS, VIRDEA

Mamma LeDeoux had a great deal to say about her form. Smyth, the great Dwarrow mechanic, had worked with the Regulus of Earth to build a titanium frame with manganese steel struts and a heated oil system carried in rubber tubes. Golem flesh made her seem like a human woman, but she was immortal and nearly indestructible. It was the first time Smyth had built a creature that was not designed for war, he had been so pleased with his creation that he had given her the services of a complete Battleunit, Seven-Six-One, the last unit ever made.

Despite having a new body, a thing to celebrate, there was a more important event. Dr. Kelle Brainerd, formerly of Earth, was being named the Queen of the Electorate of the High Meadows. The meadows, after the end of the war of the Conspiracy of the Ravens, had no desire to become a satrapy of Karkoza again. Instead, they chose independence and the formation of a royal protectorate. Kelle was declared Queen by proclamation, and in the year that her inauguration was being planned, she was the busiest person in the realm.

Agriculture reform, legal reforms, small business loans, education financing, a census, standardizing the military, building an independent police force, establishing a treasury, the list was endless. Then there was the magic.

An inauguration of a monarch often sees an amazing accumulation of power into that ruler's hand. Most monarchs greedily take that power, but Kelle had decided to perform an ancient ritual that returned the power to the land. Instead of a powerful monarch, the meadows itself would see its springs, fields, farms, and forests grow just a little bit more magical. It was like a series of small business loans aimed at slowly building an economy without inflation. Only the loan was a gift, and it was magic. To perform the ceremony, Kelle had asked Ivy to be her consort, while Rains-a-Lot and Mamma stood guard.

The only sadness came two days later when Ivy disappeared.

Mamma LeDeoux had watched as Kelle pined for Ivy, even as she concealed her feelings to the rest of the land. There was a new Yellow King; did they take revenge? No, the Rangers assured them, no one had taken Ivy from the land, and as far as the truth-sayers could say, he was alive somewhere.

So Kelle had worked, never forgetting Ivy, and in only a year, her work had wrought wonders. A new capital city, the City of Glass, was rising on a strategic point on the winding river. A court of warriors, wizards, scholars, artists, and sages was forming, attached to the university Kelle was building. The meadows were proud, poor, magical, and in every way, a reflection of their new Queen.

Still, there was the one issue. It was an hour before the Queen's inauguration when Kelle, Rains-a-Lot, and Mamma met in the Field of Larks. Kelle was beautiful in her inaugural dress, green, gray, and black, the colors of her new land, but Violet—Mamma LeDeoux—noticed Rains-a-Lot was dressed in jeans and a soft leather coat. The soon-to-be Queen hugged them both and said, "I have information on Ivy."

There was silence in the field except for the ticking of Kelle's heart and the shuffle of an impatient raven.

"The ceremony Ivy and I performed was the most magical of my life. It made me one with Virdea, no longer an Earthing. It also confirmed my love for Ivy. What it did for him, I do not know, but two days later a man in Cinnamon is said to have appeared and made threats against Ivy that were heard by someone cutting the verge. I have spent months confirming the story, and now, I have my first lead. He went to 1968 Earth in the company of the Cinnamon Man."

"Rains-a-Lot, Violet, I have the Battleunit and the Rangers to protect me. I ask that you both return to Earth for me and save my love. Help him do what he must, so that he may return to be with me."

Rains-a-Lot looked at Violet who nodded back to him. Violet took Kelle's hand and said, "Go be Queen." They both then turned and headed to the Crack in Time.

SHUFFLEBOARD SAINTS

DATE: AUGUST 22, 2018
LOCATION: SARASOTA, FLORIDA

The paper said:

> "Final Contest for August Madness: 'The Redman faces Third Army' in a duel to the death on real clay!"

It was the pamphlet we had found in the Dustin-Rhodes laboratory in Wyoming.

Akari had rented a beautiful Corvette in Tampa; she had a thing for cars and a willingness to indulge herself. She was able to drop me off at the correct address and told me she would pick me up later.

It turned out that professional shuffleboard was a rogue event. The USA National Shuffleboard Association, which holds the famous, televised championship tournaments, is concentrated in Lakeside, Ohio, Hendersonville, North Carolina, and St. Petersburg, Florida, where shuffleboard reached its nadir, plus a small number of other events across the country. This shuffleboard stadium, though, is off the map, behind the scenes, and definitely not avowed. Still, some of the champions of the more staid game crossover, and they can be said to live in two worlds: one of gentleman restraint and Edwardian rules and the other a cut-throat, combative game of precise skill only equaled by Razor-Board Luge.

Akari roared up to where my guide was supposed to meet me. My health had been failing for a while, but in the sunshine of Florida, I had rallied a little. Despite this, Akari said, "Dude, are you sure you want to go through this? Isn't the story over?"

I smiled at her. "It can never be over. It is just what I can write, and at this point, it is about reaching the end. Where did Ivy go? I think that this would be the last chapter." I reached into my satchel. Four hundred and forty-eight laser-typed pages were neatly held in a brown legal file. Two envelopes held thumb drives containing the same information. All that was needed for me was to insert any change notes, and my publisher would run with it the rest of the way. I could close my eyes and rest.

Akari fixed me with a look and then said, "Well, there it is. And off I go. I will pick you up for our flight out of TPA."

I put my book away and got out of the Corvette. My walking stick was always a pain in the ass to travel with on planes, but somehow, it had been a constant companion during my life. The split in the wood that had made it look like trash had, over the years, grown into the face of a bearded old man. In the earliest days, the split could have been anything in its topographic irregularity, but slowly, with divine purpose, it had formed the lines of wisdom that it held today.

I had finally made out my instructions for what to do when I died, which was rapidly approaching even if Akari could not see it. It had taken a long time, but I had decided I wanted bagpipes, and I wanted things entombed with me, coins, some stones of hematite and marble, images of my lost parents, and the walking stick to allow me to walk through the next life, if that was possible.

On the side of the road stood a burly old man. He was wearing jeans, leather chaps, an old-fashioned shirt that did not properly cover his stomach, and a brown Stetson. "You the writer?" he asked.

"I am. I would like to speak with Rains-a-Lot," I said.

"He is on the clay," the old man replied.

I looked around the strip of land that we were standing on. We were on Higel Avenue by a bus stop. Technically, this was Siesta Key, one of the barrier islands that protected Sarasota from Gulf Storms. Aside from a black-gated property and an open field, there was nothing that looked like a shuffleboard stadium. I asked, "How far away is the clay?"

"Here, idiot," he said. Then, he grabbed my arm and pulled me a few feet into the field.

You could still see Higel Avenue, but it was if a fog had fallen on the road. At the same time, a large wooden structure, simple but beautifully constructed, stood in the field.

The man said, "Sorry 'bout that. The rules say no one who expects to find this place will find it. Gotta happen by surprise the first time. Once it does though, most people just take the SCAT Number 11 bus from the Pavilion or Westfield Mall, depending on how far down Tamiami Trail you happen to live."

"So this is a secret?" I asked.

The big man laughed. "Have not killed anyone recently about it, you know?"

Thc man led me into a bar. It was filled with Great War memorabilia, model aircraft, uniforms, rifles, packs and load-bearing gear, along with hundreds of pictures. "Smart cookies call it the Brigadoon Effect. I ain't no smart cookie." The man sat me at a table and said to the bartender, an elderly black man in a beautiful suit, “Bénédictine for my friend here, and give me the gutter sauce.” He then turned back to me. “Name’s Stanley Goodhome, they call me a lost generation chap.” His drink, which turned out to be rum and lime juice, and the Bénédictine arrived, along with young woman wearing a beehive haircut.

“Stanley, is this a new fish?” the woman said.

Stanley sipped his rum and lime and said, “Alice Scribner, this is Nelson McKeeby.”

I stood and shook her hand. She said, “I am just back from Virdea. Wow, how long have you been on Earth?”

“I have never been to Virdea,” I said. I sipped my Bénédictine and looked at how excited the woman was. She was dressed in jeans and a t-shirt, and she seemed to be reveling in her new life.

When I said I had never been to Virdea, she cocked her head and said, “Strange to find you here, love, but come look me up if you want to stroll out sometime.”

She left, and Stanley said, “There are people from a lot of times here. As far as we can tell, hundreds of people move back and forth to Virdea each year.”

“There is an art commune…” I started to say.

“We know about them,” he interrupted me. “Refugees tend to gather in their own haunts. There are some bars. Game stores are popular, a lot of Virdea cast offs play pen and paper role playing games.”

I drank more and asked, “Shuffleboard?”

“One of the most popular sports in Virdea. Only a master of time and space can truly excel at the game, and it does not require huge muscles. Most people come equipped with enough,” he explained.

A quiet figure walked up. It was Rains-a-Lot, much older than I remembered. He looked at Goodhome, and the burly man drank his drink in a single gulp. "I will be going."

I said, "Thanks." My head was starting to throb, and my right arm hurt. Akari had been my exercise master these weeks, as well as seeing to my healthy diet, but the seizures had not stopped. The only thing that was different was that now I no longer went to Virdea as a raven. I no longer went to Virdea at all.

Goodhome nodded and left.

Rains-a-Lot looked at my eyes, then helped me to my feet. We passed the indoor shuffleboard courts, a big television room, a pachinko parlor, and then a pool area, before we walked back to a small beach with lounge chairs. He turned a chair and sat me down on it.

I could feel my breathing growing heavy. Pain now radiated through my chest, and my extremities buzzed. I grabbed Rains-a-Lot by the shirt and said, "Tell me about Ivy. What happened to him?"

Rains-a-Lot sat down on a lounge chair himself and said, "Why are you asking me to tell you a story? Are you not the storyteller of Virdea?"

"But I am dying," I said.

He nodded. "Then you can be a ghost writer."

Was that humor from the Lakota? I looked into his eyes. He had been described to me as Jay Silverheels, and he looked it but wearier and more worldly. I collapsed onto the grass where I could hear the beach and the sound of water. I felt Rains-a-Lot slowly sit down by me.

The Crack in Time was 50 years ago. LeDeoux and I went there, sent by the Queen of the Meadows in search of Ivy, her unrequited love. He had disappeared from Virdea, and no magic would find him." He paused, then said, "As the storyteller of Virdea, isn't it your job to tell this story?"

"I am not strong enough," I answered. I could see the dark, starless night above me. Wisps of clouds made their presence known only by slowly drifting across the arc of the heavens. "And a trilogy is old hat."

The Lakota, after a few minutes, said, "You carry one of the great titles of Virdea. You are followed by Akari, one of the greatest sword witches of Earth, and you carry the Grandfather stick." He placed his hand on my shoulder as pain shot through my chest. Silence strained over the night. I could feel others approach, and Rains-a-Lot said, "You cannot let a writer storm to the last chapter of the second book. It is a journey, not an arrival."

Other voices replied. My publisher and my agent seemed to be there. I could hear Akari. She bent down by me and said, "Dying for our next assignment, huh boss?"

Then I think I actually died.

BOOK CLUB QUESTIONS

1. How does the partnership of Ivy and Rains-a-Lot represent the ethos of friendship and bonding despite their different backgrounds?

2. What role does the Troubadour represent in the original group?

3. Why did the group become becalmed, and what was the reason to leave the paradise?

4. Who are the hollow men of the book, and what do they represent in modern society?

5. How can a trilogy have two books?

6. Why was the Queen called bipolar?

7. What does the Rodehouse represent?

8. Who is Darkness?

9. What is the meaning of the shuffleboard tournament?

10. Does the author really die at the end of the book?

AUTHOR BIO

Nelson McKeeby is a native of Iowa, born near Spirit Lake to a Navy Officer and his teacher wife. Placed in classes for slow learners at a young age, he was never able to make education work and left school by age sixteen. He immediately landed a job as one of the country's youngest live-air television directors and professional television writers, a career he has maintained since then. Nelson is neurodiverse with both autism and severe epilepsy. A long time hitchhiker who often uses his experiences in his writing, he has also served with the Department of Justice and as a deputy sheriff.

Nelson is known for non-fiction writing about insider politics, law enforcement, the entertainment industry, and the Quaker faith. He splits his time between La Habra, California and Iowa, living with a Brazilian doctor of biology and nurse, and four cats in a multilingual household.

More books from 4 Horsemen Publications

Fantasy

D. Lambert
To Walk into the Sands
Rydan
Celebrant
Northlander
Esparan
King
Traitor
His Last Name

Danielle Orsino
Locked Out of Heaven
Thine Eyes of Mercy
From the Ashes
Kingdom Come
Fire, Ice, Acid, & Heart
A Fae is Done

J.M. Paquette
Klauden's Ring
Solyn's Body
The Inbetween
Hannah's Heart

Lou Kemp
The Violins Played Before Junstan
Music Shall Untune the Sky

R.J. Young
Challenges of Tawa

Sydney Wilder
Daughter of Serpents

Valerie Willis
Cedric: The Demonic Knight
Romasanta: Father of Werewolves
The Oracle: Keeper of the Gaea's Gate
Artemis: Eye of Gaea
King Incubus: A New Reign

Kyle Sorrell
Munderworld
Potarium

SciFi

Brandon Hill & Terence Pegasus
Between the Devil and the Dark
Wrath & Redemption

C.K. Westbrook
The Shooting
The Collision

Nick Savage

Us Of Legendary Gods

So We Stay Hidden

The West Haven Undead

PC Nottingham

Mummified Moon

T.S. Simons

Project Hemisphere

The Space Between

Infinity

Circle of Protections

Sessrúmnir

The 45th Parallel

Ty Carlson

The Bench

The Favorite

The Shadowless

Discover more at
4HorsemenPublications.com

Printed in the USA
CPSIA information can be obtained
at www.ICGtesting.com
CBHW031944100824
12783CB00063B/232

9 798823 202381